THE MISSIONARY'S WIFE

A Romance and Spy Story
Based on Actual Events

Jonathan Hoke Barclay

Culicidae Press, LLC
PO Box 620647
Middleton, WI 53562-0647
USA | Earth | Universe
culicidaepress.com
editor@culicidaepress.com

Ames | Berlin | Lemgo

THE MISSIONARY'S WIFE

Copyright © 2023 by Jonathan Hoke Barclay. All rights reserved.

No part of this book may be reproduced in any form by any electronic or mechanized means (including photocopying, recording, or information storage and retrieval) without written permission, except in the case of brief quotations embodied in critical articles and reviews. For more information, please visit culicidaepress.com

ISBN: 978-1-68315-057-2

Library of Congress Control Number: 2023942199

Cover image © 2023 by Mike Gilger (see note on page 257).

Designed by polytekton ©2023
Some images generated by Midjourney AI system and modified by polytekton

Our books may be purchased in bulk for promotional, educational or business use. Please contact your local bookseller or the Culicidae Press Sales Department at +1-515-462-0278 or by email at sales@culicidaepress.com

twitter.com/culicidaepress – facebook.com/culicidaepress

Table of Contents

Prologue — 11

Chapter 1 — 18
Connecticut, USA, November 1937

Chapter 2 — 22
Michigan, USA, August 1936

Chapter 3 — 26
Washington DC, USA and Warsaw, Poland,
September 1, 1939

Chapter 4 — 30
Warsaw and Auschwitz-Birkenau, Poland, October 1941

Chapter 5 — 33
Wheaton and Chicago, Illinois, USA, January 1942

Chapter 6 — 34
Chicago, Illinois, USA, March 1942

Chapter 7   **36**
A Step Back

Chapter 8   **39**
Atlantic Ocean, 6:00 PM Local Time, September 5, 1943

Chapter 9   **44**
Atlantic Ocean, 6:35 PM Local Time, September 5, 1943

Chapter 10   **46**
Maracaibo, Venezuela, September 6, 1943

Chapter 11   **49**
Maracaibo, Venezuela, January 1944

Chapter 12   **54**
Club Militar de Maracaibo, Venezuela, February 1944

Chapter 13   **60**
A Step Back

Chapter 14   **64**
Quito, Ecuador, March 3, 1944

Chapter 15   **68**
Maracaibo, Venezuela, March 3, 1944

Chapter 16   **74**
Caracas, Venezuela, German Embassy, March 15, 1944

Chapter 17   **77**
Maracaibo, Venezuela, March 15, 1944

Chapter 18 78
Town of Gibralter, Venezuela, April 1944

Chapter 19 83
Lima, Peru, May 2, 1944

Chapter 20 95
Lima, Peru, May 3, 1944

Chapter 21 100
Arequipa, Peru, May 4, 1944

Chapter 22 103
Bolivian, Paraguayan, and Brazilian Amazon - Pantanal, Late June 1944

Chapter 23 109
Maracaibo, Venezuela, July 1944

Chapter 24 112
Maracaibo, Venezuela, July 1944

Chapter 25 114
Lorient, France, August 1944

Chapter 26 117
Merida, Venezuela, August 1944

Chapter 27 130
Merida, Venezuela, September 1944

Chapter 28 132
Merida, Venezuela, September 1944

Chapter 29   135
Merida, Venezuela, Late September 1944

Chapter 30   137
Merida, Venezuela, Late September 1944

Chapter 31   139
Orinoco River Mouth, Venezuela, Late September 1944

Chapter 32   145
Orinoco River Mouth, Northeastern Venezuela, October 1944

Chapter 33   151
Maracaibo, Venezuela, Early November 1944

Chapter 34   157
Maracaibo, Venezuela, November 1944

Chapter 35   161
Maracaibo, Venezuela, November 1944

Chapter 36   165
Caracas, Venezuela, November 1944

Chapter 37   170
Normandy, France, June 6, 1944

Chapter 38   174
Caracas, Venezuela, Late June 1944

Chapter 39   177
Maracaibo, Venezuela, July 1944

Chapter 40   181
Maracaibo, Venezuela, July 1944

Chapter 41   183
Maracaibo, Venezuela, July 1944

Chapter 42   185
Maracaibo, Venezuela, July 1944

Chapter 43   190
Maracaibo, Venezuela, August 1944

Chapter 44   194
Maracaibo, Venezuela, August 1944

Chapter 45   195
Maracaibo, Venezuela, August 1944

Chapter 46   198
Orinoco River Basin, Venezuela, August 1944

Chapter 47   207
Maracaibo, Venezuela, August 1944

Chapter 48   208
Maracaibo, Venezuela, August 1944

Chapter 49   210
Maracaibo, Venezuela, September 1944

Chapter 50   211
Maracaibo, Venezuela, September 1944

Chapter 51 216
The Kehlsteinhaus (a.k.a. The Eagle's Nest),
   on Obersalzberg Mountain, Germany, October 1944

Chapter 52 221
Maracaibo, Venezuela, September 1944

Chapter 53 226
October 1944

Chapter 54 228
Brazilian, Peruvian, or Ecuadorian Amazon,
   November 1944

Chapter 55 235
Brazilian, Ecuadorian, or Venezuelan Jungle,
   End of November 1944

Chapter 56 240
Maracaibo, Venezuela, December 1944

Chapter 57 242
Undisclosed Location, Venezuela, December 1944

Epilogue 252

A Note about the Cover 257

Prologue

Dear Reader —

First and foremost, I thank you for your interest in this book. Many lives crossed paths at just the right moment in history eighty-plus years ago for a story such as this to evolve into sharing with you what happened in the life of my mother Alexis, her husband Jim, and their close friends during World War II (WWII). They were part of a small team that had, what I believe to be, a significant impact on accelerating the end of that war.

Our story begins around the time the United States declared war on Japan — December 8, 1941, the day after the Japanese surprise attack on Pearl Harbor, Hawaii — with Germany declaring war on the United States on December 11, 1941.

Even before a declaration of war that many saw as inevitable, President Franklin D. Roosevelt in late 1940 was deeply concerned of a British collapse, should Germany attempt to invade. Therefore, Roosevelt had William J. 'Wild Bill' Donovan work with officials to assess the chances of Britain's victory, in case England were indeed invaded by the Nazis. William Donovan was a successful Wall Street attorney and World War I (WWI) hero who was awarded the Medal of Honor. Donovan was certainly qualified, having been an acquaintance of my grandfather Royal Hart. They fought together in WWI.

Upon return to the United States, Donovan met with the President and they determined that the British would only be able to survive with substantial assistance from the United States.

In preparation for the war that the majority thought would happen sooner rather than later, in July of 1941 Roosevelt created a civilian agency within the White House to oversee and coordinate American intelligence. Before this point in time there was no such formal agency. He appointed Donovan head of the newly created office as Coordinator of Information (COI). At Donovan's request, the US military Joint Chiefs of Staff (JCS) merged the office of the COI into the JCS, to improve trust and share military resources. On June 13, 1942, Roosevelt issued an executive order which dissolved the COI and created the Office of Strategic Services (OSS). Donovan received a commission as an Army general and became head of the new agency. The OSS was America's first centralized intelligence agency, the direct predecessor of the Central Intelligence Agency (CIA), and forerunner of today's Special Forces.

The basic mission of the OSS was to obtain information and to coordinate espionage activities behind enemy lines for all branches of the United States armed forces during WWII. The OSS specialized in dropping operatives behind enemy lines or near foreign locations of the enemy, to carry out sabotage, demolition, counter propaganda, and disinformation activities. Agents aided and supported resistance fighters as well as gathered information on enemy resources and troop movements.

Individuals were recruited for skills rather than background. Prospective members would undergo stringent mental and physical tests but were chosen primarily based on a combination of intelligence, imagination, creativity, courage, and ruthlessness. Men and women from all walks of life, from around the world were recruited, including, but not limited to, lawyers, psychiatrists, gunsmiths, engineers, chemists, missionaries, police detectives, prisoners, safe crackers, bankers, journalists, and gangsters. In addition to US citizens, the OSS trained German and Austrian individuals for missions inside Germany. Some agents even included exiled communists, anti-Nazi prisoners of war (POWs), and German and Jewish refugees.

The selection and training of candidates was top secret and was extremely rigorous. It was not unusual for only one family member to be aware that their partner was selected or sent on a mission and — as in the case of the engaged-to-be-married Alexis Hart and Jim Barclay, where each was selected and trained individually and the father of each was informed in secrecy — neither Alexis nor Jim knew until well into their marriage and mission in South America that the other was an OSS agent; an extreme and very unique situation.[1]

Additional critical information to this story is my grandfather's military service during WWI, purportedly "the war to end all wars." His name was Roy Hart. He was a tough-as-nails sergeant during the battle in France against the invading Germans, including the Battle of Cantigny near the Somme, America's first major offensive movement in WWI; the Battle of Belleau Woods, Germany's final offensive of that war, much like WWII's Battle of the Bulge where, in both cases, the Americans barely hung on; and the Battle of Meuse-Afgonne, where Roy was one of the one-million American soldiers who fought in this last and decisive battle of WWI. Roy constantly reminded his men that their job was not to die for their country, but to be sure the German soldiers died for theirs. He loved his men, and they loved him back.

On a side note, Roy's role in these battles is elegantly described in his four-page discharge papers, handwritten in cursive, that show the interesting ending to his military career that began at sixteen years of age! While volunteering to go to war and lying about his age, Roy and

---

[1] For more information regarding critical female OSS spying during WWII, please read the following *The Atlantic* article and books referred to within the article titled *Female Spies and their Secrets,* The Atlantic, June 2019 issue, Lisa Munday. In this article, note the following quotes of Maxwell Knight, an officer in MI5 (Britain's domestic-counterintelligence agency). To quote some verbiage from his 1940 memo, "on the subject of Sex, in connection with using women as agents, "one thing women could do was seduce men to extract information … what is required is a clever woman who can use her personal attractions wisely." Alexis Barclay was one who met the requirements to a 'T'.

Figure 2: Roy Hart's dog tags showing his carved name and U.S.A. on one side, and his ID number 1222965 on the other side.

all his fellow soldiers were handed thin metal tags on which to self-hammer his name and serial number (see image above)

After the war, Roy moved back to his family's home in Connecticut, married Susan, and built a highly successful business career. His biggest success in life, however — and he told this to everyone, including General Donovan — was born as Alexis Hart in 1919, the only child. Of the many positive attributes Roy and his wife taught Alexis as the three Harts grew together — referred to by Roy as 'Team Hart' — and highlighted in both word and example, were being Christian, patriotic, independent, compassionate, and strong. Period.

On July 8, 1943, and to the delight of Roy, Alexis married her college sweetheart James (Jim) Barclay. From November 15, 1943, and until retirement in Michigan in December 1976, Alexis and Jim served as highly effective, respected, and loved Christian missionaries in South America — serving in Sao Paulo, Brazil; Lima, Peru; Quito, Ecuador; Bogota, Colombia; and, Maracaibo, Maracay, San Cristobal, Rubio, and Caracas, Venezuela.

During the first four years of marriage and of their time as missionaries — and in response to a direct request from General

Donovan and President Roosevelt — Jim and Alexis served as OSS secret agents in the worldwide battle to defeat the Axis powers of Germany, Italy, and Japan during WWII. Alexis resigned from the OSS in August 1946, and Jim continued both his missionary and OSS roles until resigning his OSS position in disgust and protest after the failed Cuban Bay of Pigs incident in October 1961.

Despite my mother Alexis' "exciting but limited" (her words) clandestine work, she was very lonely and bored most of her adult life, less so during WWII of course. My dad Jim traveled abroad more than seventy-five percent of his first twenty-four years of marriage, from 1943 to 1965, most often to Zurich, Switzerland; Miami, Florida; capital cities and rural areas of almost every country in South America; all the Eastern bloc nations (covertly), and Washington D.C. Remember, this travel is mostly by air on propeller planes, before the arrival of passenger jets, and bus and car travel in third-world South America and a completely destroyed post-WWII Europe.

My mother was brought up in a wealthy and sophisticated New England family, both in Connecticut and near New York City. She deeply admired and loved her father Roy more than herself. Roy was well to do, a highly respected member the community, and a senior executive at The General Electric Company. He would not allow any products by competitor Westinghouse Electric in his home, and generally treated all the competition as he did any enemy in war.

Why would Roy always tell his daughter that she could do anything she wanted to do? Because she was Alexis Hart, that's why. Roy made sure that his daughter would be able to survive in a world where women were generally treated poorly. Alexis went to the best private schools in Connecticut, where she excelled not only academically (debate team, piano, fluency in English, French, German, and Spanish), but also athletically (archery, rifle/pistol, swimming, and horse-riding teams). She just did everything well and knew how to work at being the best. Most of all, according to Roy Hart, she learned to "work efficiently and hard, float gracefully, move powerfully, live with passion and compassion, maintain honesty and integrity, and fear God." Yes, Roy was a sincere believer in the Triune God, the strength, mercy and compassion of God, and, most sincerely, the mighty and fearful God — along the lines of American theologian Jonathan Edwards' sermon "Sinners in the Hands of an Angry God."

Finally, Roy was a fervent outdoorsman, and was himself an admirer of President Teddy Roosevelt, including Teddy's bravado, in battle and in private life, when, for example, he mapped parts of the Amazon from 1913 to 1914.[2] Roy was an avid hunter, and Alexis would be, too. He was convinced that his hunting skills, outdoor survivability experience, and general knowledge of the outdoors and its creatures kept him alive while fighting in Europe.

Roy shared with Alexis almost all he could about his "work against the Germans." He hated what he did "over there," but he did it, and did it well. For his men and himself he tried to avoid structured military warfare such as the trenches, or walking, then running toward a machine-gunning enemy across open fields. He killed German soldiers with his knives, his own pistols, and his hands. And Germans tried to kill Roy and his buddies. He condemned the terms of the 1919 Armistice that supposedly ended WWI, because he was confident the German army would be back. Because of what Roy told my mother, she strongly disliked and distrusted Germans as well — except one.

And, of course, the references above are the primary sources from which Alexis honed her competitiveness, sense of self-worth, self-confidence, "somewhat masculine skills" (for the time-period, a way of saying that she loved the outdoors, knew how to hunt and kill, but also knew her role as a woman in that society), and her natural ability to negotiate people's behavior within and outside of societal norms — particularly the behavior of men.

She adored any man who was able to face life the way she was taught by Roy. There were few of these men, and she pretty much ignored most anyway. She loved people, and they loved her — primarily

---

[2] Millard, Candice. *The River of Doubt: Theodore Roosevelt's Darkest Journey.*

because she was humble "despite all she has and is." As any beautiful and sophisticated woman, particularly a lonely American wife in South America, my mother was repeatedly courted and tempted by wealthy, charismatic, and 'dangerous' men — the kind of men she liked. Nevertheless, and despite some 'falls from grace', she held her marriage and her Christian faith together throughout.

Roy Hart died in 1956, two years after I was born. My mother died in 2010, 56 years after I was born. Both left a portion of their unique spirit in my sister and me, and this legacy was further clarified and enhanced in mother's carefully and thoughtfully written journals. A year after my mother Alexis Barclay passed at 91, I found these personal journals, and I finally would learn about parts of my mother's life that, frankly, confused my sister and me as we were growing up. I was ecstatic when I learned about my mother's mostly unknown but meaningful impact on history. Historical impact was important to Grandpa Roy, my mother, my dad, and now to me and my three daughters.

Mother was always motivating us to do something meaningful with our lives, as we felt she had done and was doing with hers — you could sense it. Mother told us that a well written and preserved life journal was akin to validating and celebrating the unique meaningfulness or impact of your life on history. She added that, unlike most of humanity which does not or cannot keep journals, labeled by mother as the "un-journaled" versus the "journaled", the written journaled naturally were more often remembered and entrenched in history as having been meaningful in their lives.

"Honest remembrance" was recorded by my mother in her journals, she was extremely proud of her life's accomplishments, and felt and acted as if her life was meaningful to every person she met — and now I know why ... and hopefully, after reading this story, you will, too.

Thank you, Mother.

Chapter 1

Connecticut, USA
November 1937

The November air was crisp and cold, as were the hunters. Five of them — Roy and Alexis Hart, leading the group, as always, and Mr. Vanderbergh, the highly successful and wealthy financier and close friend of Roy, with his twin 20-year-old sons. Each member of the party knew exactly what she or he was doing individually and as a team, and the powerful, experienced, and beautiful buck had no chance of survival.

Roy had seen the 16-pointer in these parts earlier in the week, and he wanted him badly, very badly. The two fathers and these three young hunters had constituted this five-person hunting party since Alexis was six years old. Twelve years later, they were wiser, better shots, quieter hunters, focused like hawks, and knew instinctively what each member of the party was doing — and which direction the hunted was headed.

Alexis' rifle was the .30-06 (thirty-aught-six) that had just broken the silence. Roy kept holding his rifle under his arm while he tried to light his pipe. Mr. Vanderbergh was stuffing tobacco between his teeth and cheeks. His boys were beginning to expel bullets from their rifles. Alexis stood approximately fifteen yards ahead of Roy, standing still, with her rifle remaining on her shoulder, loaded for a second shot, if necessary.

No second shot was necessary. Each of the four men looked toward the direction Alexis was now moving. They could not see the 16-pointer that Alexis had just dropped, but they all had heard the heavy thud of a large deer collapsing to the leaf-blanketed damp soil in their tree-crowded midst.

"Oh, just relax, lady," Mr. Vanderbergh blurted to Alexis. "When did you last miss?"

Roy had the proud-father smile; maybe even the my-daughter-shoots-better-than-either-of-your-two- older-sons smile.

"Done," Alexis said matter-of-factly as she propped her cleared rifle against the tree. She never kneeled for her shots while hunting. She stood tall, steady, and squeezed the trigger immediately after taking aim. She knew what she was doing and looked sharp doing it.

"None other than she," whispered one of the sons under his breath.

"Why does Alex always get point?" questioned the other twin loudly. Close family members often referred to Alexis as 'Lexi' or 'Alex'.

The three were more brothers and sister than anything else. They loved each other dearly. And Alexis certainly did not want to hear what was coming next from the proud father of the two men.

"You young men will get enough of that if you ever have to go to war," Mr. Vanderbergh snapped at his sons. "And you will volunteer for it, but you will not like it!"

Regrettably, one of the twins did not come home from fighting in World War II. The young man was a Ranger during the invasion of Normandy on June 6, 1944. He was shot point-blank by a Nazi soldier just as the Ranger got to the top of the cliff. He was dead before his body hit the beach seventy-five feet below. That particular Nazi was also killed point blank, by one of the Ranger's buddies, and was pushed to fall off the same cliff and onto the same beach.

Alexis was walking towards the deer while simultaneously pulling her buck knife from its sheath on her right hip. The buck

Figure 3: Alexis, after shooting the 16-pointer.

was still. Shot right through the heart. It felt no pain. Alexis slit its throat in one motion — letting the blood flow without clogging up the savory meat. The Harts and the Vanderberghs deeply respected the role in the universe of the hunted creatures, they killed as painlessly as possible, and ate what was killed.

Roy smiled at the simplicity of the kill and Alexis getting right down to business. All three of the young hunters were on the high school's rifle/pistol team — state ranked, of course.

"You three get this magnificent animal ready, and I will send Joseph out with the tractor and cart," said Roy matter-of-factly.

He so loved hunting with these young people — so full of life. Different from the Western front of WWI, when young American men, as old as these and younger, were placed in positions where they were mowed down by German machine guns. A tear always came to Roy's right eye when he had that thought. It was hell, and he had shared all he could bear with Alexis. He wanted Alexis and us to remember — that is all.

Finally, I failed to mention that Roy Hart entered the war as a conscientious objector who drove the ambulances — which had, as he described to mother, "tourniquets, cotton bandages, saws, and mostly dying and dead men." No morphine and no penicillin. Roy Hart's discharge papers describe battles fought and how Hart more than once dropped the bandages and picked up the rifle with the bayonet — his is not the story of the one who stuck to his beliefs while others were killing his buddies as they bled on their litters. I respect those in the war who heroically stuck with their conscience, and those who heroically could not.

This story is about souls who had to make their life-and-death decisions day in and day out. Incredible to me.

Chapter 2

Michigan, USA
August 1936

"Hi, Coach," said the cute seventeen-year-old Pontiac High School junior named Carol, as she skipped by.

"Who's that?" Coach exclaimed as he pointed at the handsome and very fast young male athlete who just sped by on the track. The kid was wearing long-legged standard white pants, a striped, white-and-blue t-shirt, and no shoes; very healthy in his summer tan.

The Pontiac High School football team had been the State of Michigan high school system powerhouse for the last fifteen seasons under Coach. That is all that kept Coach at Pontiac High — he spit, cursed and had also been, you know, divorced. Men and women who had divorced in those days were looked down on by people who had never had a failed marriage themselves or were too afraid to act on those failed marriages.

My natural mother (not Alexis) was divorced in early 1953 and, still single, gave birth to me thirteen months later in 1954, but nobody other than my natural mother and her sister knew about me or my natural father — another story. Divorce and having a child out of wedlock was a terrible black mark in those days in Maine, so I will therefore assume that being divorced twenty years earlier was at least worth two black marks, even in Michigan.

But Coach's teams won. Even churchgoing, conservative, and middle-class Pontiac big-wigs (mostly white men working in the powerful automotive industry) could look past Coach's human 'failings'. He won, and in that situation, most overlooked a 'mere character flaw' in the winner, a flaw that would otherwise be deemed a 'significant weakness' in anybody else.

"That's Jim Barclay, Coach … you know, Doc Barclay's younger son. He's now a sophomore," answered the thirteenth assistant coach during Coach's fifteen-year tenure to date.

Doc Barclay, once a pistol-carrying 'wildcatter' in Colorado, also had a winning church-growth record over all the years Coach had been at Pontiac High. Doc was the revered pastor of Pontiac Baptist Church, and at the time and by all accounts, the most respected evangelist in the Midwest. Doc was the reincarnation of Jonathan Edwards (author of the famous 1741 A.D. sermon *Sinners in the Hands of an Angry God*), and Doc had a highly visible compassion for every soul of every type, race or color … sin was sin, but Doc approached each sinner where the sinner was in life, high or low, rich or poor, black or white, hateful or lovable, kind or mean, lover of football or squash (which, as a 'little ball and racket game' Doc thought was 'for sissies'). Doc also introduced evangelist Billy Graham to the world at a tent crusade in Muskegon, Michigan. Much later, Billy slept in my bed in Lima, Peru in 1962, but this too is another story.

Doc never approved of Coach's behavior, nor did he give one 'woof' about the whispers behind Doc's back about his 'association' with Coach. Doc cared for Coach's soul, and the souls of the whisperers. Coach and Doc were an odd couple on the sidelines of every football game. Coach would curse and spit, and Doc would wince and pray.

"Crap!" growled Coach.

Coach knew all about James Arthur Barclay. Nobody on Coach's State Champs 1935 team could come close to Jim Barclay in athleticism, smarts, speed, perfect-hitting height (6' 2"), weight

(190 pounds), and 'hands'. Those hands were just as fast as Jim's feet, faster even.

"Coach, remember … he loves music, wins trombone competitions, writes music and poetry, and, I have heard through the grapevine at church, boxes down at Kelly's Bar and Boxing Club," stammered the assistant. Doc cared for Rufus Kelly's soul as well. The Black Irishman was never allowed to officially compete due to his color, but in his day, Rufus 'reduced' everybody … every challenger, every color, every race, every size, every time, in every cellar, in every part of Detroit. Period.

I never knew that dad loved and excelled in boxing, much less studied boxing under Rufus Kelly. Dad revealed this to me on a bus in Chicago when he visited me during my first year of law school. As a side note, Dad would educate me on many things while riding on a bus in a South American capital city. He introduced me to the 'facts of life' on a bus in Quito, Ecuador, while we were sitting directly behind two Catholic nuns. The nuns just happened to be from the United Kingdom, and appeared to hear every word dad spoke to me while I squirmed in embarrassment.

Anyway, dad taught me that, like fly-fishing, boxing, and fighting is an art form … and like every thoughtful act in life, the art form requires the disciplined flow of ballet, meaning that each action just made toward the competitor (or enemy) is in preparation for the immediately following action. If all the single actions are combined as one movement, that actor's movement wins, and the unsuspecting opponent/competitor/trout loses.

Coach knew that Jim would never play organized sports for Coach's, the High School's, the City's, or Jim's glory.

"Crap!" Coach growled.

"I hear the others call Jim — but never to his face — 'Hun lover', because he has befriended and 'protects' his now best friend, Jonathan Speer. You know, Speer is that 'strappingly handsome' Junior currently here for two years. His father works for General Motors, and they are here in the US for two school years. The kid is apparently a great student like Jim — he tutors Jim in German and Jim tutors Jonathan in Spanish."

"And" continued the thirteenth assistant coach, "Jim is convinced that Jonathan could out-kick any field goal kicker in Michigan, possibly the Country, kicking the football like a soccer ball. You know, with the inside of his foot for greater distance and control!"

"No kicker of mine is going to kick an American football with the inside of his Hun or anybody else's foot. Never! And no other American football player from now until eternity will ever kick an American football with the inside of his foot — it is too … feminine!" exclaimed Coach.

"Stupid looking thing, that trombone!" Coach said in disgust. Then Coach spit between the assistant's feet, cursed, fidgeted with his naked wedding-ring finger, and walked towards his feared defensive line.

"They were talking about you, you know," Carol whispered to Jim while they sat together on the grass, under the 'kissing tree'.

"I know. They were also talking about me and ever-so-handsome Jonathan Speer," Jim whispered back, in a humble yet teasing I-know-everything way.

"Lip reading again!" Carol responded in feigned disgust.

"I'm good at it, you know."

"That is what they all say," Carol said, this time with pride. Jim Barclay was a big catch in 1936 high school terms. At the time, Carol Fisher was James' flame. A year older too, much to my Grandma Barclay's chagrin. And Carol remained an important part of both Jim's and Jonathan's lives until her death at one hundred years of age.

Chapter 3

Washington DC, USA and Warsaw, Poland
September 1, 1939

It was a hot and muggy summer day in each Capital.

The main difference between the two capitals at this moment, however, was the many tons of bombs being dropped on the city of Warsaw starting at 7:30 AM Warsaw time or 1:30 AM DC time. Those were dropped by the German standard bombers and the screaming Stuka dive bombers. To make matters worse, in a few days Poland would be under attack from the Russians and certain Slovak territories which, together with Hitler and Russia's Stalin, had already divided up the spoils of the sure-to-be successful invasion.

Thousands of Nazi troops overran the significantly less experienced Polish military, and it took only twenty-nine days before the Polish government surrendered to their arch enemies.

Thousands and thousands of Polish citizens laid dead in the streets, having been killed by the bombs or the debris from collapsing buildings — or, of course, some were simply and summarily executed by the warmongering German Wehrmacht soldiers and their devil-like SS comrades. This was the eleventh time since 1553 that Poland as a country had been invaded and crushed. Number 11, however, was already the deadliest.

President Franklin Delano Roosevelt was just now getting the information that Nazi Germany had begun an all-out blitz at 7:30

AM Warsaw time. The President was livid. Why were he and his staff surprised? They all saw this coming eventually. The English Prime Minister Chamberlain was, as the President said in private to his closest staff, "an appeasement dreamer and fool." The English leader had been fooled and played by Hitler.

"We are close allies of the English. Therefore, we were fools as well," stated the President to his anxious staff.

"I want answers by 9 AM today to the following questions. Why were we caught with our pants down; who let us down over there; and what do you suggest I say to the American, Polish-American and Polish people at 10 AM today on the radio?"

"And get Donovan here right now," demanded the President in his raspy voice. The President always relied on his close and wise best friend.

"Go!"

This surprise invasion, much like the yet-to-come bombing of Pearl Harbor by another Axis power, required a strong response from the United States, but as the President often put it — delivered in a delicate way.

As Chamberlain was happily waving a piece of paper that Hitler had signed to confirm Germany's commitment to peace in Europe, the President was rehearsing how he and his country would respond to the inevitable growth of Hitler's regime and the so-called Third Reich. The President did not like using the term Third Reich because just the sound of it seemed to add legitimacy to that evil empire.

The builders of this evil empire, Hitler and his thugs, wanted to conquer the world for Germany's masses and for themselves. All empires need money and treasure to grow, and what better and quicker way than to steal treasure from the weaker neighboring countries and their citizens and then, of course, from countries around the world?

Donovan and the President then had one other significant concern about Germany — its deep and secretive relationship with

Swiss banks, particularly the Swiss National Bank (SNB). How far into this relationship will the Swiss government go? They were and are a neutral country, or were they? Swiss national and private banks ended up providing financing for Germany's war effort, and financially structured title transfer trickery that would erase a legitimate owner's identity. In today's language we call it money laundering. The Swiss money masters were eager to look neutral, at least in theory, but they were simply smart, self-serving, evasive, and often evil bankers.

There is significant evidence that Swiss bankers looked the other way as treasure from foreign nations and their unidentified citizens was smuggled into Switzerland and deposited into their bank coffers.

Incredible, that seventy-eight years after World War II, little justice has been seen in the return of treasure to the families from whom the Nazis stole everything. Of course, the great majority of these individuals were killed in Nazi gas chambers and their bodies turned to dust in the Nazi concentration camp ovens — or residents of an entire town were eliminated by summary execution and then buried.

Donovan and the President knew that throughout history, the Swiss have financed warring parties, often both sides, and played the banking and finance game extremely well to their benefit.[3] And Donovan would remind the President, "if the Swiss bankers play their cards correctly, and we all know the cards are stacked, this coming world war will provide the Swiss banks with their greatest wealth ever. When the Swiss finally realize that Germany will not win the war, their tune will change, and they will have already

---

[3] See Arons, Mark and John Loftus. *Unholy Trinity: The Vatican, the Nazis, and the Swiss Banks*; The Last Deposit: Swiss Banks and Holocaust Victims' Accounts; Ziegler, Jean. How Swiss Bankers helped Finance the Nazi War Machine; "Credit Suisse Impending Probe into Nazi Bank Accounts, U.S. Lawmakers Say," in *The Philadelphia Jewish Exponent*, April 20, 2023.

amassed billions if not trillions of dollars in funds they would launder (with included fees) or hold in secret accounts for Hitler and his thugs. Remember, the SS was structured as a self-funding enterprise — a clear incentive to take from others for their personal benefit." In other words, the Swiss bankers were money-launderers of the highest order.

No truer words have been spoken about the sinister Swiss banks and of the Swiss citizens benefiting from the success of these banks. Personally, it sickens me that more light has not been shed on the role of these banks before, during and after WW II. Shortly after WWII the US government openly tried at least three times to force these 'neutral' banks to disclose all that occurred. The banks returned approximately $60 million in 1946 — but any educated person is confident that this was just a pittance of illegal gain the Swiss banks had and continue to have.

More light is beginning to be shed on this issue through investigative reports, such as the Frontline production titled *The Sinister Face of Neutrality*, which can be found on YouTube.[4] You will learn more there than what I can detail here. Please take the time to watch the excellent production.

---

[4] See https://www.pbs.org/wgbh/pages/frontline/shows/nazis/readings/sinister.html, accessed 7 August 2023.

Chapter 4

Warsaw and Auschwitz-Birkenau, Poland October 1941

They were taken at gunpoint from the Warsaw Ghetto and crowded into the railroad box cars waiting at the station in Warsaw. The Nazi soldiers simply grabbed people and pushed them into box cars until there was virtually no room for the persons to move or breathe. When the door was slammed shut, the human beings inside were in the dark, confused, hot, thirsty, struggling to breathe, and with no ability to sit or lie down. Close your eyes and imagine the horror as you hold your imagined baby in your hot and weak arms. The only fresh air came into the boxcar through the cracks of the floor, walls, and ceiling. There was no water or food, and certainly no sanitation.

Four days later, the train and its human cargo arrived at the Auschwitz-Birkenau concentration work camp. When the doors slid open, persons dead and dying were simply pushed aside as the living struggled for fresh air to breathe — many had already died from suffocation or heart failure. The longest recorded transport of Jewish Poles to Auschwitz was eighteen days. When the Nazi soldiers opened the cattle doors, all seven hundred and fifty-eight Poles were already dead.

The remaining members of the Baczynski family, whose husband/father had been summarily executed at home for 'resisting arrest', stood in a tight group at the end of the ramp. The mother thought that the two older sons were certain to be picked as laborers, but what about herself and the three younger siblings, including the baby? A foul- and loud-mouthed SS officer, while brandishing his Luger pistol, forced the family down the station ramp to where a higher-ranking Nazi SS officer was separating those selected for physical labor and those who would go directly to the communal showers, where, they were told, they would be refreshed and reunited with their family and belongings.

The boys learned a few hours later that their mother and siblings had been summarily gassed to death in the so-called communal showers, and then cremated. The belongings were ransacked for treasure. Neither of the two Baczynski boys survived the war. The entire family was converted to dust and vanished from the face of the earth.

What follows is information that should never be placed in any person's document as an afterthought. I believe that, as a human race, we remain disgusted and outraged at the suffering that occurred during WWI and WWII. We must do all we can so that the facts and circumstances that led to these wars are never allowed to occur again. I am a student of WWI and WWII — and a student of those devastating events knows that truly, these wars together were just one huge conflict that cleared out the evil related to empires, emperors, empresses, kingdoms, kings, queens, and the highly privileged classes who had ruthlessly governed and selfishly smothered Europe's majority and their empire's even larger minority for hundreds of years. The death of Archduke Ferdinand and his wife, and the lives of German Kaiser Wilhelm II, Hitler, and their henchmen were but the pawns of fate (allowed by God) who precipitated the quick and dramatic changes in Europe and the world. At least that is my viewpoint, and that of my mother Alexis and father Jim Barclay.

If ever it seems that I make light of those conflicts in this writing, it is never intended. How could I, when the two wars I call one conflict, singly and together, were the bloodiest events that were responsible for over eighty to ninety million deaths of soldiers, non-military civilians, mothers, fathers, daughters, sons, grandmothers, grandfathers, aunts, uncles, adults, children, babies, the unborn, cousins, in-laws, the displaced and homeless, the disabled and the shunned, the gay, the Romani people, and all others society deemed at the time (and often still deems) undesirable. Imagine that during the period of 1914–1919 and 1929–1945, one of those humans was you. Imagine, shed a tear, and say a prayer for them.

Probably most importantly for the life of Alexis Hart Barclay, the awful negative events above screamed for many positive counteractions by brave individuals such as Jim and Alexis Barclay, and by so many, many more whose stories are not told on these pages.

Finally, and carefully, note that each life utilized by the OSS required ethical and moral compromises that, in the eyes of these servants, was believed to have eternal consequences. As my mother stated somberly in her journals, it is one thing to give your life for your country, and quite another to give your eternal soul as well. Those heroes portrayed here had to make decisions that jeopardized body and soul; a difficult task.

Chapter 5

Wheaton and Chicago, Illinois, USA January 1942

Jim and Alexis were the model couple at Wheaton College and then at Moody Bible Institute. Although it appears less now than in 1940, being a Missionary overseas was a scary proposition and had elements of daring, independence, and glory — and that intrigued each of these two individuals. Finally, it was also a unique adventure, and would serve as a little deviation from fighting the boredom that was sure to come with Jim tending to God's flock all over Venezuela and South America.

Jim was a sincere romantic. There are many examples in my files. For the engagement day, he printed hundreds of front-page copies of the above-the-fold headline of the Chicago Sun (precursor to the Chicago Sun Times), which announced "'Nordic Hunter Misses Aim, Gets 'Hart'", obviously a word play on their last names.

Finally, he wrote many short poems to Lexi. Below is one of the first left to me by my mother, in a chronologically ordered file:

> *September fourth a year ago*
> *You looked so sweet to me,*
> *That I determined in my head*
> *More of you I would see.*
> *October came, November came, December passed away,*
> *And all the time, I hoped and hoped*
> *That you'd be mine someday.*
>   Jim Barclay — January 1942.

Chapter 6

Chicago, Illinois, USA
March 1942

The Dean was ordered — not asked — to leave the room. The meeting began in a quiet and solemn manner — and Jim knew why. The top-secret dossier he studied all day yesterday under the careful watch of two stern G-men was startling. The report had been prepared by General Donovan — top aide to President Roosevelt and acquaintance of Roy Hart, Jim's future father-in-law. Jim and Alexis intended on getting married soon. Hitler's war machine had already invaded and conquered most of Europe and had now turned toward Russia with Operation Barbarossa. The related atrocities, many described in sickening detail in the dossier, troubled Jim more than anything.

"We really do not need to talk about whether or not I volunteer to work for the President and Mr. Donovan," Jim said to the startled folks from Washington D.C. "Of course, I do, but you need to do four things for me: 1. always take care of Alexis in every way I have listed here [Jim handed the G-woman a sealed envelope titled *Alexis Care*); 2. I must be trained better than you have trained anybody else. I want to be the complete warrior, not just the squire who carries his master's weapons; and 3. My mother must never know about this. Father yes. Mother no."

"The dean here and one other adult have a copy of these envelopes and their contents. Alexis and I leave in early September

1943. We have already committed to go to Maracaibo, Venezuela at that time."

"But you said four," quipped one of the G-men.

"Good, you are listening. Alex and I are here at this Bible School at this time, and we believe that we are here to help and love others and show them the way we believe one must conduct their soul. This is our priority, and it will continue to be that way. I struggled with this for weeks after I initially understood what you are looking for — I will be using my service to God as a cover to provide a critical service to my Country and mankind. I will in a sense be … no, I *will be* lying to those who God is using me to help. I believe I am authorized to kill because I am directed to by my legitimate President. I can also, therefore, lie for my Country. I can do this, and do it well, but I must have quality time to serve my God and His people as well. — Thank you for the time and effort to get this done for my Country."

With that, the meeting was over. Jim had done what Roy Hart told him to do. He took charge and told the government what he would do and what they needed to do for Alexis and him, before the government told him what he could do or not do, and what they would or not do for Alexis and him.

The first effort to utilize Jim and Alexis Barclay occurred when the U.S. government became aware that James (Jim) Barclay and Alexis Hart (Jim's wife-to-be) were headed to Venezuela — as missionaries no less. Persons from the OSS 'met with' (meaning, trained) Jim and Alexis separately, in secret, even from each other, many times in Chicago, Pontiac, and New York City. At the time of the last such 'visit', dad was in his last year of missionary training at Moody Bible Institute located at 820 North LaSalle Drive in Chicago, where the Institute is still located today. As a matter of record, Jim and Alexis were not the only missionaries approached for help by the United States government before, during and after WWII.

Chapter 7

A Step Back

Godless Germany planned to control the world. The gateway to South America was the planned Axis invasion of Venezuela. My parents, in an extremely clandestine way, helped make sure the invasion did not happen. Much of Germany's original world domination plans focused on South America in general, and Brazil, Argentina, Chile, and Venezuela specifically. Venezuela was the crown jewel because of its massive oil reserves — the world's largest such oil and natural gas reserves, then and now — in Maracaibo, and equally large and important other minerals in Venezuela's eastern frontier, such as iron ore, bauxite, gold, diamonds, emeralds, and some minerals that today would be considered rare earth elements, used in many advanced technologies.

Oh, yes, and one more item — natural rubber.

Germany started courting the Venezuelan government and military in 1933, well before Germany started WWII by invading Poland in September 1939. Germany had planned to take over the oil refineries on the then Dutch island colonies of Aruba and Curacao (just off the coast of Venezuela) during the invasion of Poland, so that the Poland invasion would take all the visibility and geo-political heat. Who at that time in America, other than the oil companies, even knew or cared what or where Aruba and Curacao were located? But, for reasons unknown, the plan to take over the refineries did not come to fruition.

Later, in February 1942, German forces again attempted to invade Aruba and Curacao. The invasion failed miserably, and America quickly reinforced its efforts on the seas with the newly established Naval Fourth Fleet, and on land with individuals such as Jim and Alexis, to keep the Axis powers from accessing the riches of Venezuela and the entire western hemisphere.

When mother and dad arrived in Maracaibo, Venezuela, in September 1943, German oil fields throughout Europe, primarily in the Baltic States, were burning from being bombed all day and all night by the Allies. Germany badly needed oil from sources outside of Europe. Venezuela was neutral. The prospect of a German invasion of Venezuela, where the oil was, and another attempt to control Aruba and Curacao, where the refineries were, grew daily. The Allies worried about invasion, and possible Axis commando operations to disrupt oil production and transportation to the Allied forces around the world. Everybody, including Germany and Japan, knew that without access to new sources of oil, rubber, and various minerals of note, Germany, Italy, and Japan would eventually lose the war.

The Venezuelan coast was swarming with U-boats for a year before WWII started, and that presence was even larger in 1943. At the time, there were also over four thousand German and one thousand Italian immigrants living in Venezuela. Each or both European Axis powers used some of these loyal immigrants through Operation Bolivar, which was under the operational control of Department VID 4 of Germany's Security Service, to interfere with Allied oil, rubber, and mineral shipments, and kidnap and kill immigrants, visitors, or agents from any Allied country, especially America.

But the order from Hitler to invade Venezuela never came, and those Caribbean refineries continued to run smoothly and without further incident. Venezuela continued to provide uninterrupted oil and natural gas supplies to the Allies throughout WWII — up to seventy percent of all fuel used by the Allies during the war. Germany's hesitancy to invade the islands and Venezuela earlier in the war could be considered one of the major blunders that caused Germany's second loss of a world war — or, as many believe, the invasion order was actually made, but never arrived at the German forces' headquarters in Cucuta, Colombia, on the Venezuelan border. To date, nobody knows why. I have my educated suspicions.

Chapter 8

Atlantic Ocean
6:00 PM Local Time,
September 5, 1943

The story goes that it was September 1943, and my mother Alexis and my dad Jim were, you know, newlyweds. Dad was 26, mother 24.

We know that Mother was from a so-called worldly and wealthy New England home, but dad was from a strict Baptist background that assumed most of the world's population was lost (whatever they did was wrong), and family income was dependent on Sunday collection in church. Dad's father was a well-known and respected preacher and, importantly, all three of the preacher's kids ended up being what some called old-school missionaries in South America. Meaning they were sincere, effective, and godly.

And Maracaibo, Venezuela, on the north end of the South American continent, was where mother and dad were headed on this moonlit night in the Atlantic Ocean on the blacked-out Dutch tanker Hermann Hollande.

Maracaibo is located at the entrance from the brackish and very large Lake Maracaibo into the Atlantic Ocean. It is this lake that continues to sit on top of the largest oil reserves in the world. In 1939, and due to the vast riches under Lake Maracaibo, Venezuela was the world's third largest exporter of oil, and the world's largest producer of the thick black gold.

Alexis wanted to love life and enjoy every second. As a beautiful and rich single child, her life and lifestyle always went according to plan — her plan. The man mother married, on the other hand, appeared to react to life rigidly, as if he were always on a chore for God, rather than a mission. In these first two weeks of married life, mother noted in her journal that dad either did not want to take the lead in anything or did not even know how to (which makes sense to this son), or he was afraid to not let mother be in charge (which makes even more sense to this son).

Why not let her be in charge — that is what she was used to, and it was one of the top attractors in dad's mind. He loved mother more than life itself, and, when mother would not take the lead on her own, dad deferred to her first. However, when a final decision needed to be made, dad made the decision quickly and firmly. He also took the time if he could before, but certainly afterward, to listen to mother's view and also explain his decision process (this is 1940, during the golden age of *machismo*). No matter what the process, however flawed at the time, mother had dad's back one hundred percent. It was awesome to watch what was happening, and a waste of time to try to interfere or derail the process.

Newlywed virgin lovemaking, while occupying the captain's guest quarters on an old Dutch tanker, required care. There were bunks in this suite which made lovemaking even more awkward, and kind of, as mother put it later, "desensitized the senses." Nicely put. Another 'desensitizer' was what mother perceived as her husband's sense of pleasure-denial — to assuage the guilt, she thought. Mother apparently knew how to enhance the senses, and dad had spent his life being taught how to tamp these types of senses down. This changed.

On this particular night, mother had noted in her journal that her only sex-education was a statement from her mother that "sex hurts, but as a good wife, you have to participate." Sex did hurt, but only once, and it was becoming more enjoyable and fun after that, and whether it was a necessary evil or not, dad started behaving happily in the unairconditioned activity. Mother was happy too, mostly because her husband had seemed so virile on the way back from dinner when he said under his breath that he would kill the captain if he looked at mother 'that way' one more time. Sometimes, but not often, jealousy is sexy.

The first-joint-marital-climax-ever happened that night and seemed inhumanly loud, and mother smiled satisfactorily — she did it! Which, although true, was not entirely true. Everything shook at the same time - not just the young couple, but also the bunks, the baggage, the glasses, the pillows, the tanker — wow, this is magnificent, mother thought.

Dad suddenly and instinctively knew otherwise. In one swift movement, he hit climax horizontally, and the floor perpendicularly.

And without a word, dad grabbed his boxers with his left hand and opened the cabin door with his right. He was gone.

There was a full moon that night. Dad looked port side and saw the silhouette of what he later learned was German U-Boat 375. A surfaced U-Boat next to a sinking ship generally meant one thing, and Jim hit the deck as the U-Boat's stern 30-millimeter machine gun sprayed the tanker's deck from port to stern. "You never know how low you can go until somebody is shooting at you — sometimes lower than your front shirt buttons," he remembered Roy saying.

Having learned in training that German machine gunners would count to three between bursts of automatic gunfire (their machine guns overheated too quickly), dad stood up and ran those full three seconds and dove into the radio room. "Thirty-caliber. Just a Milk Cow, effectively a submarine tanker. Only two torpedoes. We must have collided," Jim concluded. He quickly scribbled a note to the nervous radioman. "Send this immediately. There is a British destroyer that has been shadowing us since we passed Florida. They will get that son-of-a-bitch that almost sank us. Hurry!"

Suddenly, everything was silent. "Gone," Jim whispered to himself. The tanker was still floating, and Jim was now above deck

Figure 4: Jim Barclay, pistol in hand, directs other colleagues on the deck of the sinking ship in the Atlantic.

telling all in sight exactly what to do. Somehow, the boxers were now on, but slipping. One hand held up the boxers, the other hand held a pistol he had grabbed off of the radioman's table. A magnificent man Jim was — solid in action, mind, and spirit.

It was as if he had been trained for this — which he was.

Alexis had just stumbled on deck. She saw the character giving directions. Surprising herself, she was not afraid. She was, however, amazed how wonderful her husband looked at this moment. Out of character, the preacher's kid and trombone player — holding up his boxers, waiving a pistol (a .45 automatic, Military, she guessed), on the deck of a burning tanker, in the Atlantic Ocean, no less, and earlier tonight having threatened to kill the captain ... mother smiled and headed back towards the cabin.

It was as if she had been trained for this — which she was — only, she knew about Jim's training, a slip of the tongue by Roy. Jim did not know about hers.

"This married-to-the-preacher's-son thing might be fun after all," Alexis mused.

Back in the cabin, mother was safe, but alone. Dad was doing more important things, she thought. And that was the first of many times during her sixty-year marriage that mother had the same thought, indeed safe, but also alone — the missionary's wife, and her new husband was, even now, more than what 'missionary' had meant to her so far.

Chapter 9

Atlantic Ocean – 6:35 PM Local Time September 5, 1943

They were all sweating profusely.

The louder and more consistent the 'ping', the closer comes death.

The captain was quietly swearing, asking himself over-and-over again: "How did they find us so quickly. Nobody knows we are here!"

"Yes, we torpedoed the ship, but, dammit, it is still floating. Why were we called off?"

Everybody heard the 'ping', but the young U-375 submariner with the sonar headphones heard it best. His curly hair was damp with sweat, and he would be teased that the more nervous he got, the curlier his hair would become. The submariners close to the sonar man had never seen his hair as curly as it was now.

The average depth of the Caribbean/Atlantic Ocean in those parts is 7,220 feet (2,200 meters), and the deepest point is approximately 25,000 feet (7620 meters). Most German U-boats during WWII had an operating depth of approximately 230 meters (750 feet). The crush depth, where the submarine implodes due to the surrounding pressure of the water, was estimated to be between 250 and 295 meters (820 to 968 feet). A long way to the bottom.

The captain had taken the submarine as low as he dared. He knew where they were on the ocean floor map, and it was a lot deeper than 7,220 feet. 'Yes, most German U-boats have an operating depth of 230 meters, and possibly 300 had been rumored to be possible, but who really knows?' thought the captain.

"Steady at 300," ordered the captain.

The British had invented sonar, and by this time in the war, sinking German U-boats by Allied depth charge cannisters dumped into the sea and accurately calibrated when to explode, was almost commonplace. The Allied convoys taking soldiers, supplies, and material from the United States to England were significantly safer and more efficient than ever. In addition, the Navy ships blockading supplies from getting to Germany through anywhere from Portugal or Spain — alleged neutral countries — to Norway were impenetrable by German submarines; a significant change from the beginnings of WWII when German U-boats ruled the seas.

Suddenly, the pinging got louder than before and a lot faster.

'They found us,' thought the captain.

There were two loud explosions — by coincidence, one depth charge exploded close to the left of U-375, and one just to the right. Explosions at the same time.

Everything went dark and cold.

Bodies, parts of bodies, clothing, oil, and diesel fuel appeared on the surface close to where HMS Blankney was circling.

"We got him," exclaimed Lieutenant-Commander Pixley to the others on the bridge.

"Better him than us," answered Lieutenant Smith. "The American on the ship certainly knew his coordinates!"

"Unusual for an American," Lieutenant-Commander Pixley said with a laugh.

'Easy to say when there is no American around,' thought Smith.

The rest on the bridge just smiled.

They each knew that but for the Americans, British children would soon be speaking fluent German.

Chapter 10

Maracaibo, Venezuela
September 6, 1943

Alexis was tired and very hot.

"You are the missionary's wife," whispered somebody behind her.

The slight movement of air in her ear from the whisper sent a welcoming chill down Alexis' spine. It was a heavy and somewhat sophisticated sounding whisper, maybe even foreign.

Of course, everybody in the crowded bodega right outside of customs at the Maracaibo, Venezuela boat terminal was a foreigner — including Alexis and Jim.

It took over six hours for the old tugboat to pull the injured tanker to the Maracaibo docks, and, of course, the torpedo incident made the pull more difficult. Jim used the term 'injured', as he tried to calm the other passengers through the night and throughout the tug pull. Alex would hear that word many times through her life.

It was hot and stuffy, inside and out. Maracaibo rarely has a breeze, or any natural air movement for that matter. It was always as if the upper atmosphere was constantly pushing down on everybody and everything. Yes, 'pushing down' is a good description, Alexis thought.

The whisper was foreign, and the ever so slight air movement was welcome, as was, strangely enough, the strong hand that cupped her shoulder as she turned around.

"I apologize that I startled you," said the smooth voice. "My name is Major Jonathan Speer. I came to the bodega to see who is visiting this hell today. Rarely are visitors so stunning." While talking, and in a very European (maybe Austrian or Bavarian) upper-class way, he gently took Alex's arm and lightly bowed as he kissed her hand, the correct way, she noted.

Alexis certainly knew how to handle this situation — or did she? — but this was not a summer evening dinner-party on the porch in Connecticut. What was this situation anyway? Her husband simply told her to wait at the bodega where he hurriedly left her alone, without instruction, over forty-five minutes ago.

Again, all these foreigners speaking more than five different languages, all kind of tough looking, and all leering at the twenty-four-year-old American woman in her light but by now quite filthy yellow summer dress and pumps.

She was only scared twice in her life, but as of this moment, she had never been. Her father, the upper-crust gentleman in Connecticut, had always made sure of that — his only child.

"I do not startle, sir. I react," mother scolded the man. Typical of Alexis, and exactly what I knew she would write in her journal. Alexis was always desirable, elegant, and graceful — but also stern — in a disarming way.

"Yes, I am Alexis Hart Barclay, wife of Reverend James Barclay, who landed with me earlier this morning." Alex was proud to be the only bride she knew who kept her maiden name as her middle name.

"Welcome, Mrs. Barclay. The rather large diamond already told me the story," the uniformed Major Speer quietly stated.

'Thirty years old, maybe,' Alexis thought.

"Your husband asked me to attend to you while he worked on the officers in customs — poor souls. Jim is a tough negotiator when it comes to the required bribes."

Alexis adored men in well-tailored uniforms and suits, ever since the first dance at the military cadet academy near her home.

"You have met my husband before?" Alex asked in a surprised way.

The Major changed the subject quickly, as if something had been said that should not have been.

"The only drink here that is cold, or, rather, lukewarm, is the local beer. However, I understand you do not drink alcohol."

Well, Alex thought, he is well informed, but, like Jim, he had no idea of Alex's youthful past. She and her WWI-veteran father often snuck drinks of cold beer on Friday nights behind the old barn near the creek at home. He, to forget the mud-and blood-trenches, she, to keep her lifetime hero company and to learn.

Her extremely strict mother never knew, and that was half the fun. Secrets from Mother Hart became a habit and an art form that served Alexis well before Jim and would continue to do so for her until she died peacefully, with an I-know-something-you-don't-know-but-should smile, seventy-eight years later.

"Certainly, I do not, sir. But a glass of anything close to clean water would be wonderful."

"You would not want a glass of anything here, young lady," he cautioned. He lifted his hand authoritatively with two fingers pointed at the tough-looking old woman behind the counter. Within seconds, beer for two appeared, and both caressed their cool (lukewarm) bottles for a moment, then downed the beers quickly.

'This woman — an intriguing contradiction, just as her husband,' the Major must have thought. But, in an exciting way, intriguing contradictions are more attractive in a woman. He smiled.

As she drank, Alex noted that the Major appeared shocked and approving at the same time. That reaction, from him, she thought, was very mysterious, and appealing — and fun.

Chapter 11

Maracaibo, Venezuela
January 1944

Things were getting organized, but every glance around the Barclay's little brick-and-cement house screamed out "where is all the other stuff … and room for it?" Well, there was no other furniture, radio, top caliber kitchen tools and pots, piano, etc. Earlier, when Jim and Alex were preparing to move to Venezuela, Alex had complained to her father that she would miss mother and dad, but she was really going to miss almost everything she wanted to take with her.

Plus, Alex noted, pay for Jim and her was minimal — how am I going to settle-in so that people look forward to coming over, so that I can — yes, show off? Back in her 'money days', which was the term that Alex coined days before getting married, when Roy took care of everything, things she needed or wanted had a way of showing up. 'Like the horses did,' Alex thought.

Roy had told Jim that once the wedding was over, so were Roy's thoughtful and generous gifts of love. Jim was now the breadwinner — and good luck. Jim always listened attentively to Roy about everything, and Roy's statement was not a surprise. Of course, Jim had every intention of taking care of his wife and family and would not accept anything anyway — unless told by Alex to accept something. It happened all the time, but Jim never asked for anything, never acknowledged gifts from the rich father-in-law, and never said 'thank-you' regarding any such matters. These rules were Jim's prepared response to Roy's statement. It shocked Roy. He was not used to a family member not asking for, or happily receiving, something from him.

Jim lived by the above rules, before and after the marriage — except one time, and he regretted it the rest of his life.

Roy did not particularly appreciate the size and quality of the engagement ring that Jim showed Roy after Roy willingly and excitedly responded to Jim's request to marry Alex. Roy never said it — however, he suggested to Jim immediately that Roy's jeweler could "possibly give Jim a great deal".

"As a matter of fact, I was expecting you to ask for Lexi's hand this weekend, and just for fun I took the liberty to ask Harold [the jeweler] for some samples," Roy offered while Roy's wife, Jim's future mother-in-law mouthed to Jim: "I am sorry!"

Jim certainly was strong enough and had the character to immediately tell Roy to buzz off, but he did not. As in combat, do all you can to be the one who picks the time, nature, and place for battle, otherwise back off and come back later — which is what Jim did.

"What about sizes?" Jim asked.

"Of the gold band or the diamond?" Roy responded, quickly, as if the line had been rehearsed.

"Each of the five rings here are three carat solitaires, VVS clarity, three-eighths inches wide, and a 5.5 mm platinum band," stated Roy. Then, in an attempt to reduce the poorly disguised tension that Roy alone had created, he added joyfully: "Coincidently, 5.5 mm is Alex's ring size."

Jim said nothing. He took each ring, inspected each design, and picked the second to the last ring that had been laid out.

"Thank you, sir. Alexis will wear the ring proudly, although no ring of any size and quality could ever do Alexis justice."

'Wow,' Jim thought, 'that was good!' That comment leveled the playing field again. It was not the comment or awkward gibberish

Roy hated. Roy said nothing else. He did also give Jim a hug and he thanked Jim for allowing Roy to participate in the wedding in a 'small way'.

Mother Hart looked at Jim and in a very sweet and kind way, said: "Jim, we are so happy, as I know Alex will be or already is, that you will be part of this rather unique family." She nodded towards Roy. "Welcome!"

Mother Hart walked over and hugged her future son-in-law. "Jim, that is the ring that Alex chose last year when we visited Harold's store for fun. I thought you should know that. You certainly are in tune with Lexi, and you have excellent taste."

Finally, Roy outdid himself, and everybody else, with the gift from the Hart Estate of a six-year-old Venezuelan Paso Fino stallion, although the country of Colombia legitimately claims the right in horse circles to brag that this horse breed was developed in their country, all the way back to the 1500s, by Spanish conquerors.

Alex was a superior equestrian. All her riding equipment was delivered to Alex three weeks after the arrival of the Barclay family, along with the certificate of membership to the prestigious Venezuelan Military Horse Club, which allows a member to utilize superb facilities around the country, including the facility just a forty-five-minute drive outside Maracaibo.

In the early summer evening, after the joyful engagement festivities had tapered down, Roy asked Alexis if she would go on a walk with him. Alexis grabbed her father's arm and off they went down to their favorite spot on the creek behind the barn. After some small talk about the fun day, Roy sat Alexis down on the little wooden bench Roy had made for Alexis and him years ago.

"Very proud of you, my dearest daughter Alexis," Roy stated quietly as his eyes allowed a tear or two.

"You are my pride and joy, and I never dreamed that God would give me such a prize as you. You are at the beginning of a new journey, and who on this earth is more prepared than you to serve your God and your country?"

"If your mother knew about you and the OSS, the strenuous training, and the fact that I am not allowed to tell her — well, she would do to me what many Germans tried to do on the battlefield. But you are ready for both marriage and war. This is very hard for me, and even the hardened General Donovan shared a tear with me last week about my only child and daughter being put in danger's way."

Alexis began to cry as she gently took her father's strong hands, hands that had done what Alexis was now prepared to do herself — kill Hun Germans, now called Nazis.

"Father, I am so proud to be your daughter, and am ready for the challenge. But no challenge is greater than being the cause of your tears. Please take a deep breath and remember who trained me — it was you. Would you have allowed my selection by General Donovan if you were not my teacher?" Alexis said with a soft smile.

The two sat on the precious bench in quiet solitude, allowing each to absorb all the events of the day. And then Roy walked over to the old tree stump, where he had taught Lexi how to arm wrestle, and pulled out a box he had placed there earlier.

"I bought this when I was in France in 1917, before I had even met your mother." He pulled out a hefty hardcover book — it was his one copy of the original *Le Superbe Orenoque* (*The Mighty Orinoco*, not translated from French to English until 2002).

This novel by Jules Verne was scandalous even in those days — a woman heroine! Imagine! And it truly depicted the dangerous Venezuelan Orinoco that Alex and Jim were certain to deal with in the years to come.

"You already read this, didn't you?" Roy asked of his daughter with a chuckle. He knew Alex had sneaked it away to her room in high school. The fact that the novel was in French only made Alexis even more proud of her covert success.

"Yes, I did," Alexis stated proudly and with no remorse. "Twice — and you knew it!"

"The novel's depiction of Venezuela and the mighty Orinoco is correct, my dear. That is why I want you to have this. The dangers you and Jim will face will be more than what is depicted here. The book will be your constant reminder to be alert — always."

With that, the discussion ended. Alex meant to say 'thank you', but could not. Neither could speak, nor did they have to. They walked back to the house arm-in-arm — as the soldiers did in Roy's war, just before battle.

Chapter 12

Club Militar de Maracaibo, Venezuela
February 1944

Alex named her horse Trench, in honor of her father and all those who served in the trenches on the Western front for the Allies during WWI. She did not think of the fact that in competitions, *Trench* does not slide off the tongue in Spanish as it does in English. This book will also be available in French, Spanish, and Italian translations — try Trench in either one of them.

But Alex and Trench were just new on the club's internal circuit, and they had placed very well — but no all-blue ribbons' yet. As many know, in this particular sport — Alex preferred referring to these as ballet performances — everything must click. And, unless the rider and the horse can convey to each other their current mental status and physical fitness right before the ballet, the blue ribbons are far and few in-between. Alex knew this, and that persistent winning, as she was able to do with Double MidNight in the northeastern United States, is only a matter of time. Roy picked Double MidNight and Trench.

It was early Saturday morning, and because Jim was out of town again, Alex immediately went to the Club to exercise and feed Trench. The Club folks did a great job with these chores, but if you are going to build a relationship with your other half in the competitions, you need to spend time with them, very much like a partner in a marriage or a human with any living creature.

Alex looked terrific in her tight tan riding pants, perfectly starched (in this humidity) loose white blouse (un-buttoned to there), and highly polished black riding boots. If sex with a dominant partner is your thing, this would probably kill you. Every head of these beautiful and aristocratic members of the Club turned toward Alex, acknowledging and approving of her presence with a faint smile; fun to watch as I was growing up.

As an important aside, Alexis was not able to become pregnant. Jim and Alexis adopted my older sister in September 1950 — five plus years after the allied victory in the Pacific, when Japan's elders finally surrendered three days after the second atomic bomb was dropped on Nagasaki.

The causes related to Alexis' alleged infertility were many. First, it is difficult to do what Alexis was required to do for the government if she were pregnant. Also, Alexis had no doubt she could not at least attract some man all the way up to birth, but it is not a situation she wanted to be in. Second, and this was troublesome latter in her marriage to Jim — he was almost never home. Truly! Mother's journals, especially for the time after the spy business was done, showed me a sound resentment towards dad for not fulfilling his role as the male sexual partner. Some lines in a June 1979 journal state flatly: "[I]t remains difficult for me to look lovingly on Jim, with all his positive attributes, when throughout our entire marriage to date, he has rarely been home, and when home, does not understand that sexual intimacy is a MUST. If he had been home more often or for longer periods of time, I could have had the indescribable experience of natural motherhood." Finally, there were no tests at the time that would without a doubt lay the infertility blame on Jim.

My sister and I spent a lot of time analyzing mother's journals. We always tried to dissect sentences and words as if through our mother's eyes — to see the statements in the time and under the circumstances they were made. The above statement hurt neither my sister nor me. We both feel that we were treated by everyone as mother's own. We were told early in our lives that we were adopted — and that, among many other things, made us special because we were chosen, we did not just appear, and you take what you got. Crudely stated, but it worked for my sister and me.

Alex checked the club's daily journal just to see if a member named Jonathan Speer had signed in. Everybody was required to sign in. She would have asked either one of the receptionists at the entrance or one of the many guards at the various guard houses around the Club, but she feared being the pursuer. The work that Alexis is being paid for, and any relationships required for that role, are more successful if she follows the norms of the country she is in — of course. Maracaibo specifically, and South America in general, was and continues to be a machismo-based society. Although times and behavior towards women have improved for South America, male dominance continues to be the desired and accepted norm, by both sexes. Unabashed acceptance of male dominance as the norm was not Lexi's strength.

Major Jonathan Speer was a member of the Club as well. As a new member, Alex had difficulty finding anything out on when this Speer guy was at the Club, if ever, and did he have a horse and stable similar to Alex? She just could not get the Major out of her mind, a condition even Alex told herself was dangerous. The picture of the handsome face, perfect hair, masculinity, and command of the situation remained in Lexi's mind for a long time — it had been four months since her arrival in Maracaibo.

And apparently Speer was not at the stables today. Alex decided to whip through everything except her time with Trench and get back home. This being the weekend, she wanted to go through her mail pouches that would arrive from the U.S. Embassy at 8:30 PM sharp — as always. If the recipients for the planned mail drop were not present and accounted for at that time, all kinds of whistles go off and mandated actions are taken. Those are very difficult to stop once they are going, which alone is capable of blowing your cover.

Alexis turned the corner towards the stables complex and stopped short. There was a figure of a man leaning on a wood fence watching a horse at one of the stables.

"It has to be Jonathan! Whoops, I called him Jonathan!" Alex gasped under her breath as she reached her right hand to her heart. "So, he does not always sign-in as required (rebel!), and he does have a horse!"

Alex began to walk again towards the stables. She had decided to say hello to Jonathan — why not. She was introducing herself to everybody in an effort to gain a certain level of comfort. As she approached, she had decided on a kind-of-surprised-and-aloof methodology. Just as she was about to pass Jonathan, she exclaimed: "Oh, what an absolutely beautiful horse!"

The gentleman was a little startled and turned towards Alex.

"Oh my, I am so sorry for interrupting your time here. I thought you were somebody else. Oh my!" said Alex as she reached out her hand to the man.

"Is it possible you were looking for Major Jonathan Speer?" asked the gentleman.

Alex was visibly shaken a little for just a second. "Oh … no! For some reason I thought …"

"Well, the man you thought I was is my cousin Major Jonathan Speer. This happens all the time. He insists it happens because he is so much better looking, charming, and mentally more stable than I am — but he loves to fantasize about love and life, so I just leave him alone," said the man joking.

"Well, I still apologize. I just met Major Speer when my husband and I first arrived at the docks and customs in Maracaibo. He was there because he was bored. We met in the bodega while my husband, who Major Speer apparently knew, was doing the 'customs thing'. Alex was more relaxed now, and slowly grabbed the fence to help stabilize herself. 'How could I have made such a mistake. But, from behind, I would swear it was Jonathan, I mean, Major Speer,' Alex thought.

"Honestly, this does indeed happen all the time. Imagine how tough it is on me when beautiful women — none as beautiful as you — keep thinking I am he? How do you Americans say — I am not just chopped liver! Is that correct?" The gentleman asked.

"Well, let me say this" — Alex was now stabilized — "you are each very, and I mean *very* attractive. Your uniforms look identical as well. You are the same height, rigid — as your uniform requires, and I would guess equally as brave on the battlefield," was Alex's attempt to flatter this man.

"Well stated, ma'am. My name is Captain Stephan Schneider, and I am indeed the Major's cousin. We not only grew up together, I lived with his family most of my early years. People thought we were twins or plain old brothers. We get along well, although we are very different in certain ways," laughed Stephan.

"Well, it is a pleasure to meet you, sir," said Alex with a slight curtsy. "As you properly guessed, we are on different sides, if you will, in this awful war. The problem for me is that it is not difficult for me to imagine my husband and me having dinner with you and your family — so long as no politics are discussed," Alex said in a playful manner.

"No family … yet," stated Stephan.

"Well then, that makes it easier. Two against one. We may make you American!" Alex exclaimed.

"Too far and too much, Alex," Lexi said to herself as Captain Schneider recoiled.

"Not likely, Mrs. Barclay," said Captain Schneider defensively.

"Well, it was indeed a pleasure to meet you. Welcome to this very comfortable country, dismissing the heat and humidity, that is," said Alexis carefully. She remained calm and continued "Thank you, Sir. I am pleased you were not Major Speer … now I know two handsome 'enemies' in Maracaibo. The word 'enemies' in quotes, sir. I am not a military expert, nor do I try to analyze someone's ideologies. Life is too short and too fun. I leave the fighting to others. I hope to see you again, maybe you will participate in some of the competitions," hinted Alex.

"I heard some members saying that you are an excellent rider and sit well in the saddle," Stephan responded. "How long have you been riding?"

Alex had already begun her move towards the stables and Trench, while she replied competitively with a "since before I was born."

"Oh, by the way, I understand your horse's name is Trench. Tough to pronounce well in Spanish."

"Yes. My father was a decorated hero in the first big war. He told me about the trenches. So, I named this horse in his honor and in the honor of all who fought in those awful conditions for an unknown or non-understandable reason — other than, of course, to stop your country from continuing to invade France," Alex said as they were each going somewhere else.

"For sure," remarked Stephan uncomfortably.

"Who won?" teased Alex.

"Nobody," replied Stephan very seriously.

With that, it all ended, and the two parties moved on.

'This is one amazingly strong woman,' thought Stephan to himself.

Chapter 13

A Step Back

A pause to remind the reader that I am the son of the missionary and his wife. There were some very personal human activities of my mother's that are difficult for this son to write for the public to see. The affair with the German Major was certainly one of them. The fact that mother killed men was another.

The last for this book is the secret sexual side of Alexis Hart Barclay.

In this day and age, what I discovered and will share here are hardly unique — but, remember these events occurred in late 1939 thru 1954 — the dark ages as far as today's human sexuality is concerned.

And, finally, during the time of the events described here, Alexis was a beautiful and sexy woman in her mid-twenties to mid-thirties — on her own over seventy-five percent of the time.

Despite all that was visible on the outside (the worldly woman), Alexis thought that it must be true that it is acceptable that a woman masturbate in the privacy of her own bed, and certainly in whatever bed she and her lover were in. However, what Lexi had to overcome was her sincere belief that sex was not a sin within a marriage, that sex outside of a marriage that was sanctioned by your government was not a sin, and sex by herself to stay sane was also not a "sin".

She did not have anyone to seek for comfort in these matters, unlike today.

She did, as did Jim and her father Roy, seek comfort in the King James version of the Holy Scriptures.

Next came the writings of John Calvin, the theologian who played a major role in European Protestants breaking from the Catholic Church in the early sixteenth Century. There are five principal points to the so called Calvinism, which can be easily researched by the reader — in fact, my suspicion is that many of the readers of this little book are protestants and therefore have at least a notion of the strict doctrines of Calvinism.

Finally, Roy had told Alex about an up-and-coming Christian intellectual named C.S. Lewis (1898—1963), who just happens to be an author whose views about life and faith my sister Zoe and I favor. C.S. Lewis was one of the intellectual giants of the twentieth century, and arguably one of the most influential writers of his day. The beauty of his writings and thought is the sincere simplicity he uses to convey intellectually complex Calvinistic doctrine.

And hence we arrive at Christianity, sex in and out of marriage, sexual roles, and, unavoidably, solo sex or masturbation.

There are so many complicated theological and practical issues here that the reader may have already laid this book down. We will not go there other than to pay honest respect to the fact that Alexis Hart Barclay, being raised in a strict Christian tradition, had to deal with issues emotionally and spiritually in her early adulthood that few, if any women, dared deal with, or admit to dealing with. This part of our story is about the relationship with Major Jonathan Speer, outside the marriage to Jim Barclay, but the length it takes to tell this story make those events with the Nazi Major appear more frequent than they were. Even though, she was a young, beautiful, sexy, religious, and yet realistic woman. She was truly someone special, and I admired and continue to admire her through every thoughtful and conscious step in her complex life. I'll end this matter with a wise snippet from C.S. Lewis regarding how his generation faced the above issues.

> *It would seem that Our Lord finds our desires not too strong, but too weak. We are half-hearted creatures, fooling about with drink and sex and ambition when infinite joy is offered us, like an ignorant child who wants to go on making mud pies in a slum because he cannot imagine what is meant by the offer of a holiday at the sea. We are far too easily pleased....*
>
> *I think our present outlook might be like that of a small boy who, on being told that the sexual act was the highest bodily pleasure should immediately ask whether you ate chocolates at the same time. On receiving the answer "No," he might regard absence of chocolates as the chief characteristic of sexuality. In vain would you tell him that the reason why lovers in their carnal raptures don't bother about chocolates is that they have something better to think of. The boy knows chocolate: he does not know the positive thing that excludes it. We are in the same position. We know the sexual life; we do not know, except in glimpses, the other thing which, in Heaven, will leave no room for it.*
>
> *It is a mistake to think that some of our impulses — say mother love or patriotism — are good, and others, like sex or the fighting instinct are bad ... There are situations in which it is the duty of a married man to encourage his sexual impulse and of a soldier to encourage the fighting instinct. Strictly speaking, there are no such things as good and bad impulses. Think once again of a piano. It has not got two kinds of notes on it, the*

'right' notes and the 'wrong' ones. Every single note is right at one time and wrong at another.

Now, try to guide my mother to daily understand how her complex physical, sexual, marital, spousal, emotional, and spiritual behavior should be, based on a situation evolving from, encouraged and sanctioned by her government, which by God's grace and instrumentality, is crucial in saving the world from the tyranny of the 'godless' Axis powers of WWII.

Chapter 14

Quito, Ecuador
March 3, 1944

Jim stepped out onto a sidewalk near the U.S. Embassy in Quito, Ecuador, adjusted his tie, and kept walking. He was planning to catch the 11:00 a.m. flight tomorrow morning back to Maracaibo. He had failed to let Alex know he would be home for dinner tomorrow night. But maybe Jonathan will tell her — he had asked him to get a message to Alex if possible.

Jim and Jonathan had been working on a quick project together. Although they worked for different bosses, they had developed a very strong personal relationship dating back to Pontiac High School.

'Somebody who should not know knows about this secret entrance,' Jim thought as he discreetly adjusted his pistol and the dagger stuck in his belt. He looked good and he felt good. This young American had just left a four-hour secret session with those in South America who reported to him and with those to whom he reported. A small, very smart human, somewhat kind, and deadly fellowship of spies.

'Deadly, of course. The enemy is just as deadly, and I always must think that I am more capable, more deadly, than my adversary,' Jim thought.

When you do what Jim was doing, you must always be extremely aware of all that is going on around you. The word 'alert' works, but Jim did not think that word had enough impact to justifiably and adequately describe the situation he and his new wife are or could be in at any given time.

Roy had shared six principles of life that he wanted Alexis and Jim to know from his life.

1. ***Stay alert***, *so you see and can take advantage of potential or existing positives, and navigate around or through potential or existing negatives (personal and business life).*

2. ***Stay relevant*** *in everything you do — work and play. You know your existence is important and valuable, so act like it. For example, if your work and efforts are not deemed relevant to you and/or the person you report to, move on.*

3. ***Nurture*** *critical relationships — to have a 'nurturing' relationship, A must want to nurture B, and B must want to be nurtured by A. And, at the same time, B must want to nurture A, and A must want to be nurtured by B. What relationship is 'critical' to be nurtured, and what 'nurturing' should mean in that relationship, often changes... so you must be alert as to when those changes need to happen, or if they have already taken place.*
ALWAYS take the time to care for, 'nurture', and feed your soul.

4. ***Think beyond*** *— when you decide to act on a matter, consider the positives and negatives that could occur after the act is completed, i.e. what consequences are beyond the act's horizon. Also, when somebody tells you that the most useful form is a square, always consider whether the form would be more functional as a circle, and vice versa, i.e. see beyond the other person's horizon, where she may not have thought what was 'beyond' what somebody taught her was a square. It is possible,*

after your consideration of what is 'beyond' the square, that the square is indeed the most useful form. But then, you made the functionality decision, not the other person.

5. **Live with passion** — *every millisecond on this earth could be your last. Remember this, not as a negative, but as an incentive to squeeze in one more positive act, toward yourself or somebody else.*

6. *Finally,* **live with compassion** *— nobody is as fortunate as you are to be you. Every person at every level should be treated with respect — even an 'enemy'. Respecting your enemy is the first step to defeating him or her... if that is something you decide to do after you think 'beyond'.*

Jim had arrived at the Embassy to practice some of his self-defense moves and behavior with the top two hand combat Marines stationed in Ecuador. Surprisingly, the Marines, tough critics who they are, only had to remind Jim of some tricks with his British made dagger. Jim preferred the dagger at any time it was an option — razor sharp on both sides, small enough to hide, so easy to work with that almost all those he had used it on, never saw it coming — and they knew Jim had 'a knife'. Jim knew he needed to get some rounds off from his M-1 Garand and his Colt .45 pistol, somewhere.

It was early afternoon on a Wednesday, the hottest time of the day in Maracaibo. At this moment he was glad to be walking in Quito, which has an elevation of 9,350 feet above sea level. It was almost always comfortably cool and dry — year-round. He stopped at a bodega for a cold glass of mango juice, and he began to think of the devotional he would use at his church and with the worshippers this coming Sunday. Jim was a devote Christian man, Baptist even. He used to complain as a young man that there were more things he could not do than there were things he could. Of course, this South American continent is ninety percent Catholic, and again, he is the 'outsider' in so many ways.

Jim always smiled when he had the following thought — 'but Alex is Presbyterian.' They are more general in their interpretation of things, still devote, but there was some 'wiggle room', using Alex's words for this topic. Jim loved his wife so very much. He was sure that Alex was a terrific lover because she was Presbyterian rather than Baptist. She was his partner, the "other him" — again as Alex would say. There was a natural ability to 'stay in tune' with each other — even during this War.

Jim knew he was gone too much. Boy did he know! A young, pre-marital virgin, in his second year of marriage gone from his wife over a planned seven months of the year. Again, it is what it is. "God is in control, and no matter what I do or how I do it, the result will be what God had planned all along. This line of reasoning helps me deal with all this," Jim concluded.

"I just need to do as well for God here in South America as I do when I am chasing those Nazis, or they are chasing me." Jim smiled, and instinctively adjusted the dagger. He had heard that Alex was going out with newly found friends this evening, and that is why he took tomorrow's mid-morning flight back to Maracaibo.

Chapter 15

Maracaibo, Venezuela
March 3, 1944

Sometimes, you just do what you want to do, damn the consequences, if any.

Alexis was surprised in herself that she was here, but not really. She had thought about this for a long time. Jim had been gone again for two months, with no word on where he was. He was likely in Switzerland about a month ago, but then the next message was sent from Sao Paulo, Brazil. Sao Paulo? Jim did not speak Portuguese. Or did he? Too many surprises with this man. Probably also speaks Japanese, she thought!

Yes, she got notices that "I am fine", "Very busy here, but thinking of you," "I cannot wait to hold you again" etc., etc., etc. All via U.S. Embassy courier, all unsigned, all suspicious. Alexis had not planned on a life like the one she was living right now.

But then she did not know of any other twenty-four-year-old woman from Connecticut who lived in South America. And, a spy! Living an adventure! Many would say a dream. Or a nightmare?

'Look at me,' she thought. She was dressed in a breezy lacy light blue dress; white pumps which matched the white hat; nylons even. Nylons, like car tires, were very hard if not impossible to find anywhere in the world these days … but Jonathan had them.

Jonathan could, very quietly, get anything. Who is this man? He has perfect taste.

She was about to find out.

Just three days ago, she was buying brooms from a young man on his donkey. Brooms did not last long on concrete floors, in high humidity, and they were poorly made anyway. No air conditioning. She was hot, sweaty, tired, dirty, and grumpy.

And then a clean, shiny black car pulled up to the new Barclay residence. *No* cars pulled up to the Barclay residence, at least not fancy ones, and clean ones. Not in this neighborhood.

But it did pull up, and out stepped a perfectly dressed, clean-shaven, handsome Venezuelan man, with a black leather portfolio. He walked directly up to Alex.

"Buenos dias, Mrs. Barclay. Very hot, muy, muy caliente, isn't it?"

Alex just nodded, as she tried to clean off her dress, dry her sweaty wet hands, and ruffle her hair.

He reached into his portfolio and handed her a crisp light grey envelope, sealed with a black eagle stamp, hand addressed, black ink in script, very nice.

"This is for you, from Major Jonathan Speer."

Alex, who still had not said a word, certainly remembered Major Speer. Who would not? Of course, he relied on that, which she immediately did not like. She had not heard a word from anybody for the first three months in Maracaibo. Nothing. Not from anyone.

"Major who?" she asked, knowing the answer.

The young messenger acted surprised and then nervous.

"Are you not Mrs. Alexis Barclay?" he asked.

"Si, I am. MRS, I remind you. I do not accept messages from other men, even a General!" She shoved the un-opened envelope back into the stomach of the startled messenger, turned around sharply, and went into her little, dirty, humid, hot, still disorganized home. Lonely too. She forgot to slam the door … for effect, she thought. She smiled.

Ten days later, mother was feeling pretty good. Of course, she thought about Major Speer, who would not — man or woman. He was beautiful. He seemed like he controlled the world. At least to her. Still nothing from Jim. Nothing. She would get used to this somewhere down the line, but not yet.

On the eleventh day after the first message effort, mother was walking home from the open market. She was getting more comfortable in her environment. Sure, everybody stared at her and whispered little somethings behind her back. It did not bother Alexis … she was taught to believe that such activity was just jealousy, and she could do nothing about it anyway. She was 'the best' person there, and she knew it and she lived it. Always gently smiling when in public, and never acting or looking 'weak'. Much like Jim and the Major, she thought.

As she turned the corner to her house, she immediately saw the black, clean car. She did not act surprised … she wasn't … and kept her same walk toward the house. "Another note", she said to herself. "Hah".

The same young man stepped out of the car. Same suit. Same tie. Still sharp as can be.

"Mrs. Barclay," he said gently. "I have something for you … again."

"Another envelope … from some man?" Mother asked.

"No … solo un hombre. Es algien bien importante quien me va a matar si te enojas conmigo".

And of course, out stepped Major Jonathan Speer. Perfectly attired. Perfect face. Perfect body under the perfect uniform … 'even if it was German,' Alexis thought.

Now, Alexis lost her composure. Literally … and unusually.

"This man is a walking air-conditioner" Alex said in disgust. If the roles were reversed here, she would be nervous, sweating up a storm, brushing away the bugs, the comb knotted in her hair, and her make-up dripping off one side of her face.

He said nothing, but walked up to Alexis Barclay, clicked his heels, and took the groceries out of her sweaty arms.

Mother said nothing. The Major said nothing. The young man returned to the car. Mother and the Major entered the Barclay residence and, without much thought and almost automatically, closed the door.

'You. Here? Why? I mean, how dare you? What do you think I am? Who do you think I am? This is scary. I am a Missionary's wife! Perception of spiritual perfection is critical! Open that door!' She thought.

The Major put the groceries on the small kitchen table.

"Alexis, it is good to see you. I apologize for surprising and bothering you."

"Open that door right now!" Mother said. She would not be in the home alone with another man, other than Jim. Never!

"You are not a bother. You are an invader ... so German of you!" mother scolded.

Now that had to hurt him, she was sure of it.

He winced.

"That was not kind ... but considering things ... I accept the statement."

"Alexis, I am here because Jim asked me to contact you. The note that I attempted to have delivered to you was from Jim."

All at once mother was embarrassed, angry, surprised, upset, stunned, mad, ... and impressed.

"Is Jim ok? Where is he? When is he coming home?"

"We think he is in Peru, in Lima. But we do not know for sure."

"We?" Alexis asked as she collapsed into the one chair in her living room. Dust rose from the chair.

"Alexis. Alexis. I am sorry."

"Why in Lima? Do you know?"

"Alexis, remember, Jim is on the 'other side'. I do not know what he is doing, nor do I know what his agenda is. He contacted me, as a friend, to tell you he is fine, he misses you, and he is doing what he has to do and is doing it where he has to be. That is his message. I know nothing else."

"Do you know when he will return?" Alexis asked in dismay.

"No," the Major replied. "May I have some water? It is awfully hot in here."

"I am sorry, Jonathan," Alexis said in a tired voice. "Of course. It is next to the stove."

The Major poured a warm glass of water and sat on the kitchen stool.

Everything was quiet. Alexis looked at the ceiling. The Major looked at Alexis. And so they sat for about a half hour. The Major had not opened the front door, and Alexis did not care anymore. 'Why should she?' she asked herself. 'Am I really married? Am I really a missionary's wife? Who did I marry? What missionary travels the world and leaves his wife alone? Not just any wife … ME! Am I a wife?'

A slight breeze came through the small open window. It broke the stillness.

"Alexis, I am so sorry. I am certain *this* is not what you expected when you came here. Is it?" the Major asked. "Alexis?"

"Oh Jonathan, I am so confused. So tired. So bored. So ugly. So lonely." Alexis mumbled.

'What did I just do?' she asked herself. 'I called him Jonathan. I told him what I just told him. I am a lovely and lonely woman in my twenties, and I have not been with a man for such a long time? Why do I think this way?' she continued. 'I am a Christian missionary's wife! What is wrong with me? There is nothing wrong with me! I am a woman, and I am young, and I am so confused! But a Christian cannot be this way. That is not what I know, or at least that is not what I was told.'

"Oh my," Alexis said. "Thank you, Major, for coming here and sharing the message with me." Alexis said as she sat up and gathered herself.

"Thank you, Alexis, for letting me in."

"I did let you in, didn't I? And you never opened the door. Shame on you!" Alexis teased.

"Next time, Alexis, if I send my messenger, please accept what he delivers to you. *And*, be nice about it. Your behavior last time was badly done," he scolded her.

"I will. And I am so sorry you had to come all the way out here from wherever you live. Where do you live anyway?"

"I live downtown Maracaibo at the Crillion Hotel. Top floor … and there is a breeze." It seemed as if he was bragging.

"Oh, no wonder your clothes are so clean and perfect! Electricity and lots of fans?"

"Yes," the Major said, as streams of sweat moved down his face, down his neck and into his collar.

"Oh, what is that like?"

"Heaven," the Major said as he walked out and closed the door behind him.

Chapter 16

Caracas, Venezuela, German Embassy
March 15, 1944

"She is the missionary's wife, for goodness sakes," an exasperated Jonathan said to his colleague and cousin. Not his 'friend', his 'colleague' — already too close of a description.

"Yes, but she is a beautiful woman, she is smart, she is American, she knows how to shoot, she is the complete package, but she is another man's wife, and she is ten percent Jewish," Schneider scowled.

"I will not respond to that last part, you scum."

"You better, and you better respond correctly."

Jonathan stood up, walked around the long table and directly toward Schneider. Schneider did not move.

They were both stubborn and brave men. Neither was afraid of anything. Each had been weak only once, and it resulted in something they did not want to happen. The common cause — a woman.

From the back, they looked like twins. From the front, they looked like brothers — Jonathan was drop dead handsome, and Schneider was devilishly cute. They could be brothers in every other sense. But, they were not, and each was glad there was no direct relation.

Jonathan outranked Schneider, but Schneider was more manipulative of the people in Berlin. Schneider played the game often and well, whereas Jonathan played the game rarely and poorly. Schneider was feared, Jonathan was respected.

"Ok, what does she know?" Schneider asked less aggressively.

"She knows nothing and will forever know nothing. She is my toy, and I am hers. That is it!"

"When you say it that way, it is easier to accept ... and it is more believable, my dear cousin. Spoken as a true German officer," Schneider marveled, jealously.

"How is Chloe?" Jonathan asked. Chloe was his youngest sister, eight years old when he left Germany for this dusty hell. Angelic face, a smile to die for, and severely retarded. Chloe loved Jonathan without question. Jonathan would die for Chloe. Maybe Schneider would too — but Chloe was more of an embarrassment to Schneider.

'Arrogant fool!' thought Jonathan.

"I love her as well, Jonathan. The family must remain cautious and alert. Very alert. She must stay out of sight, at least for now. These are bad times at home, and Hitler is lashing out at everybody. An Allied invasion somewhere in Europe is a certainty; Russia is taking charge of the Eastern front. Bad!"

"Where are you going from here?" asked Jonathan. The attitude was more relaxed, and they began to act like the family they were not.

"Now to Iquitos, and hang out there for a while. The rubber must be harvested, pressed, cut to order, and delivered to Montevideo exactly three months from now. *Must* it is. Personally, I think, this will save the Reich. This will starve the Allies. This will slow things down. We will return to South America, and it will be the breadbasket of the Third Reich."

"Breadbasket and pipeline, cousin." Jonathan always put more emphasis on the critical oil.

"But, where is the financing? Where is the gold? I can do this just on my good looks ... but not you!" Jonathan made an attempt at levity, but it did not work.

Two gold shipments have gone missing. Not funny at all. And, as far as Berlin was concerned, nobody was beyond suspicion — including Speer and Schneider.

Chapter 17

Maracaibo, Venezuela
March 15, 1944

When Jonathan returned to his apartment in Maracaibo, he was deep in thought.

Nobody knew about the shipments; only he and Schneider — and only Hitler and Himmler in Berlin. How could both shipments go missing? Maybe one, but both? There is always the likelihood that a U-boat could have just sunk. Most U-boats were dangerously capable of sinking on their own — as any historian knows, many Spanish galleons carrying tons of gold to Spain from Peru just disappeared — or did they?

'Schneider certainly has the low ethics and some stupidity to think he could get away with stealing gold from the Führer,' thought Jonathan, 'but he just could not pull it off.' He had told nobody. Nobody. He never wrote anything down. He did not date, he did not … "Sleep around?" Jonathan asked himself. 'Oh, oh,' he thought.

Chapter 18

Town of Gibralter, Venezuela
April 1944

Wednesday night was considered date night, and the date was to assist in Wednesday evening services at the small church in Gibraltar, Venezuela, about seven miles south of Maracaibo. Nice drive, clean air and always an adventure, e.g., a flat tire or ingesting interesting food.

There also have been some issues in the outer margins of Maracaibo where Calvinist theology and protestant church behavior were looked upon with great suspicion by the established Catholic church.

Being a protestant missionary in South America was a not an easy job, and Alexis and Jim attacked the effort thoroughly. They were well versed in Catholic theology and doctrine. They were facing a church which began its missionary service in South America with the conquistadors of the early 1500s — Francisco Pizarro (Incan empire), Hernan Cortes (Aztec empire), Pedro de Alvarado (Mayan empire), and Diego de Almagro (Chile).

I grew up basically afraid of the Catholic church, and with good reason. That church got there first, and its many followers at the time were concerned and afraid of the many changes that a less structured Protestant belief system may bring.

Remember that beginning in the early 1500s, the actions of the aforementioned conquistadors were closely in tune with the accompanying Catholic clerics. They had to be, primarily because that same church was itself sanctioned by the powerful Spanish Crown – and it was the Spanish Crown that ruled South America until the days of liberation led by Simon Bolivar. Forces led by Bolivar (the "George Washington of South America") liberated the territories of New Granada (Colombia and Panama), Venezuela and Quito (Ecuador) in 1819 and 1822.

It was the Spanish Crown that lost its influence when liberation occurred — not the Catholic church. That same Catholic church has remained the single most influential belief system in South America. This is true in part because the Catholic church, by default, is still the single largest landowner in South America, and it is therefore the greatest beneficiary and influence over all economic and political activities in the region.

However, it is clear that the sincere efforts by my parents and many others over the years have helped bring about a certain religious freedom in South America. And a person would be hard pressed not to acknowledge today that the continent, the countries, and their citizens have benefitted politically and economically on the current world stage thanks to this religious openness.

Nevertheless, the strong Catholic influence, even in 1943, made being a protestant missionary in South America dangerous and challenging — almost as dangerous and challenging as being an OSS agent for the United States. Not surprisingly, the Catholic church liked to keep things just the way they were. They knew the protestants would start 'causing trouble' soon, and they were aware that 'Protestant freedom' would be a costly proposition for the Catholic church.

Alex, Jim, and others had been physically threatened as well as had demeaning events such as being recipients of pots of urine sprayed over them. However, Jim and Alexis considered the source, their considerable personal love to the South American people, and the fact that they truly were on a mission from God.

They had their limits, however.

Figure 5: The scene in the church just before Jim is shot.

On this Wednesday evening, Jim was the guest speaker and Alexis and Jim played some trombone, piano and accordion. The people certainly knew about these instruments but had never seen this use of them before. Alexis loved the accordion, and always enjoyed it when she had to play the awkward instrument.

Jim had translated some hymns into Spanish, added a little local rhythm to them, and people loved it. The full church was a good testimony to this fact.

In the middle of one such hymn this Wednesday evening, however, a group of angry men (equality of mind and purpose was the Protestant message), entered the back of the small church, guns in hand, aimed at Jim singing and shot.

Jim fell to the ground. Everyone started screaming. Alexis too was now on the floor. She looked at Jim grabbing his left arm and evaluated the situation. She immediately crawled to the side exit door, opened it, and let it close. Within forty-five seconds, Alexis had moved to the back of the building, and jumped up right in front of the shooter who was sure he had seen this same woman leave the church screaming just a moment earlier.

She had not left, and Alexis certainly would not scream!

Before the shooter knew it, Alexis had grabbed the shooter's Garand, ejected the remaining bullets in the chamber and the six-shot magazine and handed the empty rifle right back to the shooter.

"Whoa!" the shooter and his kindred spirits must have thought. If she did what she just did, this woman could have killed them by now as well. Alexis looked deeply into the embarrassed and flustered man's eyes, and asked "Porque?"

The three remaining armed men were somewhat stunned, as Alexis stared the shooter down and then headed back to the front of the church to check on Jim, who was by now standing up and holding his bleeding left shoulder. Alexis sat Jim down, ripped his shirt, plugged the hole, and by now somebody handed Alexis some water.

The worshippers began to ask in unison "Porque?" and pushed the four assailants out the back of the church, and then the congregation returned. Jim made a few statements about how God expects us to love our enemies, and he added that we should also remember their names (an attempt at humor). Alexis and Jim put their materials together and headed to the small local hospital.

The above event took place in the span of about fifteen minutes. As Jim and Alexis drove away, the congregation was singing in unison a song of forgiveness and love. That is why Jim and Alexis came to South America — what a difference compared to killing Germans.

Oh, and the police never came to investigate. They knew exactly what had happened and who was responsible — the local Catholic priest.

Chapter 19

Lima, Peru
May 2, 1944

About an hour flying time out of Lima, Peru, Jim woke up with a start. He was dreaming about what he and Alexis called a 'guilt dream'. Jim felt tremendous guilt about those he either killed or significantly hurt. He knew he should not feel the guilt — he killed at the direction of his government (the most Christian Nation at that time). He counted about twenty-six individuals he killed to date — twenty-five men and one woman. In one year. That is too much. Yeah, but just one is too much. Most of the kills were very close, with the slit of a very sharp knife — and Jim always felt he could feel the soul leaving the body, and he swore the body got heavier, not lighter as most expect — a very strange and meaningful event that Jim hated.

"What right do I have to kill these people? I guess I kill to save the lives of others — those in the concentration camps in Hitler's Europe; our men fighting in the South Pacific, Europe and many other places, like where I am now! It is not fair, it is awful, and I hate this — but I am surprisingly very good at it. Is it God giving me the mental and physical strength and wisdom to accomplish my government's mission here on the earth, at *this time*? I can feel it! But how can a man, who accepts Christ and the teachings of the Bible, kill, deceive, manipulate, cheat, lie, hurt, maim, and knowingly break God's and man's laws all day long? I wish I could talk to Alexis about this ... but, of course, to do that I need to get home!"

Jim shook his head, got up from his first-class second-row aisle seat, and visited the rest room. He saw a very tired man in the mirror. Here he was only twenty-six years old, and he swore he looked old — like maybe even thirty! He washed his face and hands, and wished he had time to shave and look a little more attractive. When somebody expects you at the airport, and looks forward to the too-handsome Jim — even he could look bad! The mirror does not lie!

Marcia Bradford would be on the open terrace above the door leading to customs from the airline's rolling stairs.

"Oh Marcia," Jim gasped. Wow! An original and biblical temptress. And a truly brilliant mind.

Throughout South America during the war, little has changed; there was no consequential middle class. You have the rich and the very poor in Bolivia. Not much in between. In Venezuela, especially because it had a strong dictator during the war who appeared to care for his entire flock and wanted everybody to have at least 'something', there was a growing middle class. The rest of South American countries just had flat-out 'rich' and 'poor'.

And then, there was Marcia and her family. They just seemed to have their hands in everything of value throughout South America — most of which Marcia's brothers and her father stole directly from the national treasury of the respective country. Much like how the royal families of Europe borrowed, lent, stole money, and sexually transmitted diseases just before WWI. But oh, so much money.

"How will I do this on this visit?" worried Jim. What he really meant was how would he *not* do it this time.

Marcia was truly what most men (even women) would consider heaven's gift to a 'defenseless' human and the innate desires for love, companionship, challenge, coaching, direction, wisdom — and, of course, sex.

She wore many hats and carried out sophisticated disguises over her rather short time in the business of manipulating a man, a woman, the fortunes of either, and war. Marcia was at this time the War Consultant/Emissary to the Swiss Government. She spoke various Swiss dialects, German, French, Italian, Japanese, Chinese, and perfect midwestern English. She had studied psychology, international law, and business and law at Cambridge. She had studied international law at the University of Chicago. All this by the age of twenty-five, but she was now Jim's age. Jim would always smile when he would watch Marcia read a book or a document. Her eyes would move very quickly, like a typewriter at high speed, and she not only would read, but understand and memorize, the critical lines on each page.

'Too smart and clever for me,' Jim thought. Just being near her for dinner and drinks would strain every nerve ending in his brain, and he was always wiped out by the time he got back to his hotel room in wherever — including here in Lima.

Jim and Marcia had met here several times during the last eight months. He always had the same hotel, room and food at each hotel he stayed at in his travels — including the famous Conquistador Hotel in downtown Lima.

Jim loved Lima even more than the famous cities in Europe and the United States. Lima was the capital of the Spanish empire. All the Spanish galleons traveling from the 'new world' back to Spain, left from the port city of Callao just outside Lima. They would use street-quality bricks from Spain as the ballast and stabilizer for the trip to Callao from Europe. Those bricks would be replaced by heavy cargoes of items demanded by the aristocrats in Spain, Portugal, France, and Italy. The most precious cargo was, as you know and expect, countless bars of gold and silver, along with Inca artifacts encrusted with astonishing and priceless jewels and stones not already known by those who could afford to buy them.

As the capital of the Spanish Empire ever since the mid-1500s, the homes for the upper class had ornate wood terraces, porches, and balconies carved by Inca and Spanish artisans. Many of those items were already well over three-hundred years old in 1944.

And Jim loved *anticuchos* (grilled marinated beef heart on a stick), and *ceviche* (marinated, not cooked over a stove, white fish), along with many different spices, peppers, tomatoes and onions. Incredibly good and, more often than not, very safe. Jim had gotten terribly sick from a few servings of these famous Peruvian delicacies — but he felt it was worth it.

The plane landed hard, and Jim sighed in relief that his traveling was done — at least for the next three days. Then, back to Quito, Ecuador, then Bogota, Colombia, and then a DC-3 to Maracaibo, Venezuela — and back into Alexis's arms, and their bed.

Right after that thought came the vision Jim had thought about earlier. There was Marcia. Not on the airport observation deck, but at the bottom of the stairs as Jim un-boarded the plane. Only she could arrange that, and she did.

Marcia jumped up and down and waved elegantly. Jim felt parts of his body tingle that had not done so in some time.

"Oh my, God, help me," Jim whispered to himself as he walkded down the stairs, took off his hat, and plunged into Marcia's arms. She liked plunging. Jim knew that, and if he did not cooperate, his trip would be considered a waste, because an unhappy Marcia would not share the secrets Jim came to Lima to hear.

"Darling! Oh, you look terrible! But I like you that way sometimes!" exclaimed a happy Marcia.

"You are always my vision, Marsh," said Jim in a gentlemanly way.

Marcia's right hand deliberately and lightly rubbed up against Jim's pants zipper, and, because even holy men are still men, Jim's involuntary muscles between his legs tingled again and started filling up.

"Yes, my Jim. It still does not take much!" teased Marsh.

"Ugh!" stated Jim, as a defensive effort to slow things down.

"I am so glad to see you, Marcia. You hear it all the time, but you are absolutely stunning and seductive. Amazing woman you are," Jim exclaimed. He knew every single man getting off the plane, including the three Catholic priests, envied where Jim was right now. And Jim did enjoy the jealousy of others.

Alexis, Marcia, Anita, Soledad, and my dear Emma (the Finnish wonder), Jim was amazed by his luck. Each of these five women was convinced that Jim should have married her.

He automatically used his left fingers to confirm that the wedding ring was gone. He had stuck it in the coin pocket of his suit pants. He felt his pants to confirm, and, yes, his ring was there.

Jim and Marcia walked into the terminal and were waived directly through customs.

Outside, at the curb, being watched closely by a smartly uniformed military officer, was Marcia's blue and black BMW 335. This convertible car was manufactured in March 1939, and production was then stopped in early 1941. Only four-hundred were made during that short time period, and how Marcia got her hands on this one, in Peru no less, was, in Jim's mind, the eighth wonder of the world.

"I love this car, dear Marcia. It fits you … and me, by the way," exclaimed Jim as he tossed his small Austrian suitcase, his Italian hand-made brief case and his English-made hat into the tiny back seat. Marcia beat Jim into the car, and the second Jim sat down, they were already about twenty-five feet from the curb.

"I want this … and you!" whispered Jim into Marcia's cute right ear.

"I do not blame you," challenged Marcia. The wind blew back her thick blond hair.

"You are flawless!" Jim yelled over the increasing wind as the couple sped down the road to Lima.

"I know!" replied Marcia, very confidently. "I am still working on you, old man."

Jim was two-and-a-half months older than Marcia, hence the name-calling.

"Not too old, however," tempted Marcia.

Jim winced but was able to crack a pained smile as he made some physical adjustments.

"Feel better?" Marcia teased.

"Ugh," was the response.

The drive up the small hill to Marcia's home was always a treat. She owned the entire hill — all fenced-in with black Italian iron bars, a guard at the gate. As the guard waved Marcia and today's 'boyfriend' through the entrance, Jim looked at the small steel rods sticking up slightly from the grass at the bottom of the right gate column — three of them.

'Good,' thought Jim.

Marcia lived well, very well. Her family — very influential in the quiet circles of families who run the world — lives on a mountain in Switzerland somewhere. That is a story in itself, but not for here. Suffice it to say that nobody, and I mean nobody, would dare harm Marcia in any way (no matter what regime, family, religion, or country); you are signing your and your family's death warrant to harm her. Hitler knew this, as did the SS. Roosevelt knew this, as did the OSS. The leaders in Japan knew this, as that is all that mattered in Japan. Mussolini knew this — and he was advised bluntly by Marcia's family to not court her. Jim and Jonathan knew this. And Marcia knew as well.

The home was built in a very one-story-concrete-with-stucco-South-American way. The rooms surrounded an exotic and well-manicured garden and sitting area within an expansive yet cozy courtyard. Fans and beauty everywhere, including Pete and Sue, the two peacocks. Every window had the black Italian iron rods embedded in the concrete walls. Only two exterior doors — both on either end of the West wall. Bulletproof. An always occupied guardhouse at each entrance. Each guardhouse was at least as well stocked with weapons as any armory in South America — maybe not as many weapons, but at least close to one of each.

Figure 6: The courtyard in Marcia's house.

It was nighttime, so it took Jim a moment to look up in the courtyard. Darker than usual, he thought.

"Marsh, what did you do?" Jim exclaimed in awe.

The ceiling of the entire courtyard, a ceiling that once belonged only to God and His creation, was now laced with the same ornate iron lattice on all the windows and the garage. Beautifully done, but just not the same.

Jim looked at Marcia in surprise and some disgust.

"I know, Jimmy. I know. It takes something away," whispered Marcia.

"It takes away everything," Jim fumed.

"A gift — or should I say demand — of the Führer," chirped Marcia.

"Why would you …"?

"Because Jonathan said we … and I mean we three… had to. Everybody has their eyes on the German and American Embassies in downtown Lima. I store 'stuff' … Marcia put up her fingers in the quote symbol … for the Reich, and for other countries such as our USA. And others. My beautiful airy starlit courtyard in my beautiful home now is more secure than any embassy or bank here in Peru."

"Probably more like Fort Knox …" Jim muttered.

"The Reich and Jonathan, huh?" Jim said, loud enough for Marcia to hear the disgust in his voice.

"Oh, come on, Jimmy. It is only gold, weapons, cash for use in any country here on the continent, some documents, maps, I will never look at, and …" Marcia stopped.

"What?" Jim asked impatiently.

"Juicy fruit, Hershey bars and M & Ms," Marcia responded affectionately. Yes, she knew all about Jim, and she adored teasing Jim about American chocolate.

"Hah. And I bet Jonathan brought you the candy to store for me." Jim's tone had gotten a little better, but he was still annoyed. He was maybe a hero sometimes, but sometimes jealousy between

Jonathan and Jim could be cut with a knife. In this case maybe the sharpest sword, right now.

"Well, yes, but only because I told him to bring a bunch down from Washington, D.C. a few months ago. I keep your habit and weakness well stocked. And I reminded him of the Toblerone chocolate you had brought him from your last Switzerland trip."

"Yeah," said Jim in resignation. Marcia had him pegged. She knew things about Jim that sometimes Jim had forgotten about himself.

"You know, Jimmy, even the Germans have tried as hard as I to figure you out. I read the dossier that Jonathan had on you. He does not know I read it. At least I do not think he does. You two can fool even me sometimes. You were wiser than Jonathan when you just shared what the OSS knows about Jonathan."

"Why do you call me 'Jimmy' and I never hear you call Jonathan 'Jonny'?" Jim asked as if annoyed. He knew she did, but he hated to hear why.

"Because the names 'Jimmy' and 'Jonny' are terms of endearment — Jimmy. I love you both — equally."

Jimmy, Jonny, and Marsh had had this discussion together in Jamaica last year. That love triangle is a story in itself, and the complexities would take several well bound large books to sort out. That dinner under the stars in Ocho Rios, Jamaica, was a night that will be etched in the minds of each of the three forever. Maybe even the last thing each would see flash in front of their eyes when death finally wins the battle.

Suffice it to say that morality was grievously wounded that evening. The three did not end up in bed together as Marcia had somewhat kiddingly suggested as the evening wore on. Neither Jim nor Jonathan cared about each other that way and, to be frightfully honest, Marcia did not want either one using her for comparisons to the other women they have had — including Alexis. Neither would win, and that would only drive them away from Marcia.

"Damn that German spy," cursed Jim. Yes, he was jealous that Jonathan was only committing fornication, but Jim was committing adultery, and of course, because there was a spouse involved, adultery was far worse. In this regard, Jim being the minister of the group, generally held back on some of his more intimate activities with Marcia, but he certainly never shared that with Jonathan. And Jim was always conflicted with the act that whatever he did *not* do, God knew that Jim certainly wanted to 'be inside', so Jim might as well, he and Marcia would sometimes reason (either individually or together in a moment of passion) but he never did. Kind of like the question — if I slit the man's throat and he dies within minutes, that for sure is killing. But, if you injure the man gravely, and he dies three days later, he is still dead, but who or what killed him? To Jim's annoyance, Jim knew that the time of death would matter neither to God nor Alexis. At least in a separate breath, Jim would end the guilt session with the thought that true all-the-way-lovemaking was another thing Jim would certainly beat Jonathan at, but Marcia will never know. Yuck!

Marcia loved Jim, and Jim's best friend Jonathan. But this was true of many of the women who knew both men well. Jim was loyal to his lover, who happened to be his wife, Alexis. Jonathan was loyal to his lovers from many countries, when he was in those countries, and that included Alexis in Venezuela.

"So, when did you last see Jonathan?" Jim asked, almost as an afterthought.

"About a month ago," Marcia replied directly. "He was worried about you, Jim. He said you have been traveling so much that his men sometimes lose you until you show up somewhere where you want to be seen — most recently Switzerland. How do you do that?"

Jim had by now taken off his tie, his shoes and unbuttoned the top button of his suit pants. Being around Marcia caused Jim much temptation and discomfort. He was human, for goodness sakes, and long flights make most men yearn for sexual release. He would spend all his time in Marcia's presence making adjustments — and Marcia enjoyed the game.

"Beautiful flowers, Marsh."

"From Jonathan's mother," Marcia quipped. "Well, truthfully, the flowers showed up at the same time the doily under the flowers arrived from Jonathan, so I guess he knew the flowers were coming and wanted to get some credit as well. The doily is so delicate and tasteful. Such good taste."

"Ok," Jim acknowledged. He knew Jonathan had tasted the lovely dessert of life that Marcia was … and Jim knew he never would. He was proud of his honor, but there was a price, and that was the discomfort.

The breeze from one side of the house to the other was always the same — perfect and dry. All curtains were wide open all the time. There was no building or elevation of nature that was higher than the foundation of Marcia's home for over seven miles — exceeding by far the sniper distance challenging the safety of Marcia or the identity of any of Marcia's guests.

"Truly the safest place on earth," Jim whispered to himself.

"Jimmy?"

"Nothing … just finally relaxing."

"Why are you here … other than, of course, to see me?"

"The German's need almost everything right now, and South America has all of it, and more. You know this. But there is one thing they need now more than ever."

"Gold," Marcia and Jim said together.

"And they cannot mine it here yet. They need a large cache to take and buy the Third Reich's place in history."

"Atahualpa gold — right?"

Even then, many had heard of and tried to find the fabled cache of gold the Incas assembled to pay Pizzaro the ransom for the Inca Sun God."

"Anything in the wind Marsh?" Jim calmly pleaded.

If Marcia knew anything, she would always tell Jim. Why? Neither Marcia nor Jim really knew. They were just that way with each other — they were 'one' the moment they met. Marcia, who kept and told secrets from people all over the world, never lied to Jim, and vice versa. They shared everything — except love-making.

"I want you inside me someday Jimmy … I know I have to wait another lifetime."

"And I the same lifetime, my dear Marcia."

"How is Alexis?"

"Lonely, as am I."

"She is a beautiful and elegant woman, Jimmy. I envy her to the same extent she distrusts me."

"She respects you, Marsh, and trusts both of us. She wants your life, and I do not blame her. We have not made love for over three months. It is hard … I mean, difficult."

Marcia caught the joke.

Chapter 20

Lima, Peru
May 3, 1944

"I assume the weapons got here in good enough shape," Jim was talking to Marcia with his mouth full of warm, salted-butter-fried ripe plantains (*platanos* in Spanish). This was Jim's all-time favorite food, and Marcia knew it, as did her staff. She kept a constant supply of these delicious cooking bananas for Jim whenever he was in Lima.

"I had no idea how large those things are. We were sent five of them — the new U.S. M2-2, your original U.S. M1A1, the U.K. so-called 'Ack Pack', none of the three Russian versions and, of course, two of the German 10 models — of course, since they invented those things, theirs are better than all ours," replied Marcia in disgust. Marcia worked with the Germans some, but she clearly hated them.

"Anyway, all of them are in the weapons silo over there." Marcia added.

"I never understood why your weapons-bombs-ammunition silo is in your courtyard, Marsh, unless just to keep track of them."

"Bingo!" exclaimed Marcia, much to Jim's annoyance.

"How about us taking a trip up into the mountains and test them out? Could we leave later this evening? And which of your vehicles do you recommend we take this time?" Jim asked. "We need cargo room, but more importantly we need power and speed."

"We will leave in about three hours. I will have the men stock us up with all we need — including ripe plantains and butter, and our side weapons," Marcia offered. "We will take the black Oldsmobile 76."

Jim was delighted. The Oldsmobile 76 was light, powerful, and fast. Marcia loved cars, and had the vision to have her guys place a modified V8 in the 76 (the Oldsmobile 76 was the predecessor to the first true 'muscle car', which was introduced to the American public in 1949 in the form of the Oldsmobile Rocket with the high-compression overhead valve V8).

"And about six hand grenades, please," Jim added.

Although fire has been used against enemies since the beginning of warfare, it was not until 1913 that a German inventor (those Germans really liked hell-like toys and creative ways to kill others) named Richard Fiedler improved and refined a weapon that emitted pure line-like flame towards the enemy. The weapon was first used by the Germans on WWI's Western Front — and at first, the French were so shocked that they just ran. Who would not? However, the French quickly recovered and quickly regained the trenches that had been lost.

Of course, by the time WWII rolled around twenty years later, the Allies followed suit, and the United States used the flamethrower to great success in getting the Japanese soldiers out of miles and miles of underground tunnels and caves during the battles in the South Pacific — particularly the battles for Iwo Jima and Okinawa.

The basic concept of the original German flamethrower was to allow the soldier to spread fire against the enemy position by launching a pressurized concentrated jet of burning fuel — either diesel fuel or napalm gel. However, the gel and the mechanics behind the flamethrower had never been tested at the heights where battle might occur in South America. Jim and Marcia had been ordered to take these weapons up into the Andes to see how the various flamethrowers worked in the high altitudes where Arequipa, Cuzco, and Machu Pichu were located, approximately eight thousand feet above sea level. The U.S. think tanks were certain that if the Nazi's were successful in winning the war in Europe, South America would be the next continent to conquer — with all of South America's weak armies, high-level governmental naiveness and corruption, and, of course, oil, iron ore, gold, silver, rubber, diamonds, etc.

It was a relaxing, if curve-filled, drive. Jim was at the wheel, and he sure loved this upgraded Oldsmobile, and was looking forward to the new Oldsmobile Rocket 88 that he knew was coming but was delayed because of the war.

Marcia, on the other hand, hated the curvy roads and took a few special pills so she could basically sleep the entire time.

The quiet is nice, thought Jim, and certainly better than pulling over every hour or so for Marcia to throw up. Marcia also suffered from thin-air sickness, and on these mountain trips she kept with her a small oxygen canister with a small tube that she constantly held under her nose.

This was easily a sixteen-hour driving trip from Lima, Peru to Arequipa, Peru. Arequipa is approximately 7,500 feet above sea level and used to be the capital city of the Spanish Eastern empire. Jim loved spending time in the city and in its fine hot-springs resorts. A big fan of white-anything, Jim loved the fact that all the older city buildings were built with *sillar*, a local white volcanic stone. There are also beautiful Spanish churches still standing from the time of the Spanish Empire. The Catholic church ruled absolutely everything of consequence — San Francisco (1552), Augustine (1574), and La Compania (1552) — and the National University of San Augustine, founded in 1828, a catholic university where Jim had participated in debates regarding Calvinist theology and Catholicism; fun debates and Jim loved the challenge.

As he pulled up to the Plaza Central Hotel, Jim took a deep breath and looked forward to sit in the hot springs and just relax. His shoulder was feeling a lot better after the church shooting in Venezuela, and he felt he was back in so-called fighting shape.

The couple stayed in the same suite, but with separate bedrooms. The hotel was known for the luxurious care of its tenants, and Jim and Marcia enjoyed the scenery from the fifteenth-century balcony overlooking Plaza Central and Misti Volcano. There are three dormant volcanoes in Arequipa, and always a risk of earthquakes.

It was a Sunday morning when Marcia woke-up, rinsed off, and crawled into Jim's bed with her bathrobe.

"Your still wet, pretty lady," Jim feigned disgust.

"You are complaining?" mused Marcia as she loosened her robe to expose her delicate yet firm breasts.

"Cover those up! I cannot think while I gaze at your perfect frame and make comparisons to the perfect Oldsmobile Rocket 88. I want one!"

"Stop it, and you can have these two right now! How can you dream about cars at this moment, and do not compare my body to that of a car, and from Detroit no less. And the car is not even on sale yet — believe me, I have checked and checked. They are keeping it under lock and key. How do you know about it?"

"I should not have asked," pouted Marcia.

"Secret!" bragged Jim.

Marcia caressed her cup of fresh Andean black coffee. "I want to just stay here all day and recover from the trip. Ok?"

"Certainly," replied Jim, as he worked his way out the other side of the bed and headed into the large marble restroom connected to his room.

"Boy, if these walls could talk! Imagine, since 1550, dignitaries from here to around the world have rested — or not — in these very rooms. Amazing!" Jim observed. He loved this spot on earth, and what man would not be proud and excited — yes, excited — to have a woman such as Marcia attempting to seduce him.

"This man is that man," Jim said to himself as he thought of Alexis and looked at his image disappear with the vapor from the shower fed by the hot springs.

"This man what?" asked the naked Marcia as she entered the roomy shower with Jim. There were six shower heads each aimed perfectly at the two marble chairs facing each other in the middle.

"… is tired," quipped Jim.

"Not according to that," Marcia joked as she pointed toward Jim's groin.

"I know." Jim said in a calming and loving voice.

"Mr. Barclay always takes the longest showers up there," Alfredo the desk manager said as he watched the hot-water level in the hotel's vast hot-springs caldron head towards 'very low'. "We will just charge him the 'over-use' fee again. He never complains. Also, I like his Venezuelan wife better."

Chapter 21

Arequipa, Peru
May 4, 1944

Jim and Marcia were exhausted. The two Nazi pursuers were gaining on them.

"Lie down here. Now! Act like you hurt your ankle! Hurry!" Jim almost yelled back to Marcia. Marcia quickly let herself fall down at the end of the bridge and yelled out in 'pain'. The pursuers had just come around the corner on the other side of the bridge. Jim still could not be seen, and Marcia continued her charade related to a broken ankle.

"He left her?" asked one man to the other.

"Pig that he is! Well, we have her now. Go get her!" commanded one pursuer to the other.

"Really? When I cross that bridge, I will stay on that side for a long time. I hate these rope bridges!"

The man was referring to the already famous Q'eswachaka rope bridge, initially created by the Incas over five-hundred years ago to cross the treacherous Apurimac River. "One hundred-and-fifty feet of fear," Jim used to say. "It moves. It sways. It bounces. But it remains and has been constantly under the care of the local Quechua Indians for hundreds of years. Safest bridge around!" Jim would yell back at those who he convinced to follow him across.

Figure 7: The Q'eswachaka bridge under flamethrower fire by Jim.

"Let's get her. Think about the torture and the reward!" one snarled at the other as they began to cross.

"Jim?" asked Marcia rather loudly. She had not seen him for a minute or so, and she was getting a little nervous that he had fallen off another cliff or something.

As the men got near mid-point — out walked Jim with the USA-made flame thrower in hand.

He whistled to get the pursuers attention, smiled broadly, and pulled the trigger.

"Go to hell you Nazi-Hun pigs!" yelled Jim.

The faces of the men told the story. They saw the flame, knew they were in hell already, and going to a place much worse. They yelled, screamed, and cried as they saw the gel-fed flame devour the north end of the bridge. Jim, a man with little mercy when it came to Nazis, finally aimed the flame right at the men. The dry rope burned even more quickly than Jim had calculated.

The movement of two desperate men on the bridge only hurried the ultimate end. Within seconds the bridge snapped, and each man, already on fire, fell to his death over a thousand feet below.

"Too much drama for me, Jim," Marcia mumbled as she got to her feet and brushed-off the dusty grass.

Jim looked tired after the fight. He just sat there and pushed the empty flamethrower over the edge.

"How do we get back?" Marcia almost pleaded.

"There is a nice solid metal bridge down that way about two miles. Can you make it, or would you rather wait here for me?"

"In this situation, dear, you are going nowhere without me. There are Nazis everywhere here. That was the last of the flamethrower tests, and fortunately the last one worked well up here too. Let's go back to Lima now!"

Chapter 22

Bolivian, Paraguayan, and Brazilian Amazon - Pantanal Late June 1944

Jim had barely recovered from getting Marcia back to Lima when he had to head into the Peruvian and Bolivian plateaus and marshes to meet up with Cheo and his cohort Ruth. Ruth was as tough or tougher than Cheo, and Cheo knew it. She was also extremely attractive with her DNA mixture of Spanish, Brazilian, English, and Portuguese decent. Jim and she had a pure business relationship.

Alexis never met Ruth.

On the Pantanal Cheo, Ruth, and Jim were to meet with local tribes who had been watching for German spies or sympathizers — all on the look for the famed Inca gold. It is always dangerous to enter and exit — if you do — the Pantanal.

This area of Bolivia, Paraguay, and Brazil remains highly unexplored, and many believe that the Inca gold is in Pantanal — one of the last unexplored regions in the world. These same people also believe that the gold will never be found — but, it is there, Jim thought.

Other than the many still-to-be found tribes, Pantanal's most lively inhabitants include dangerous black jaguars, giant anteaters, piranha, howling monkeys, and green anacondas—the world's largest snakes, which prowl swamps and lazy rivers in search of wild pigs, deer, and other prey.

Figure 8: A South American black panther lurking in the jungle.

'Other prey' had included some humans.

Jim hated going into the Pantanal — even worse than Cheo and Ruth did. That could explain why they were not thinking well when they were captured.

Things had not gone well on this trip into the Pantanal.

It is rare that three tough-minded explorers such as Cheo, Ruth, and Jim would fall into a stupid little trap like the one they did just now.

"Stupid of each of us! When we get out of this, we need to review how we got here," Jim whispered to his two equally wiped-out partners.

The situation did look rather grim this time. Hopefully, the other two had the same thoughts.

"Just like Jim to find the lesson in this — as a preacher would and should. He also is always so sure things will work out ok, we just need to think hard."

"And they should have stayed more alert," another word that Jim will whack the other two with, "when we get out of this."

The three had just finished a thirteen-mile hike back into and out of the Amazonian rain forest onto this beautiful and peaceful Bolivian or Brazilian or Paraguayan landscape of Pantanal. To this day the countries have not yet settled where their borders meet.

When the three foreigners entered the Bodega Central, aptly named for this little town because it was the only one here, the regulars eyed each very carefully — the guns, the knives, the boots, the belts, the ammo bags and clothing, all made in a place called 'Made in USA', just like the labels for the other groups of strangers who visited, but never left, these parts during the last five years.

"Whatever this Made-in-USA stuff is, everybody uses their stuff, so it must be worth killing for," were the thoughts of at least the leader of the four Andean hoodlums now restraining Jim, Cheo, and Ruth. To their dismay the three held foreigners also saw the United-States tags hanging from the belts of each hoodlum.

Jim began trying to reason with the men in Quechuan, but he ended up having to speak Spanish *and* Quechuan to get the message across.

"You must be in charge here, and good for you. Leading a group of men such as these most certainly is considered an honor in these parts. You do not have to be rough with us at the moment. As your men are honored to be led by you, we too are honored that it took men of your caliber and toughness to finally be able to catch us."

The two men pointing rifles at each of the three strangers smiled a mixture of glee and evil.

'Not doing such a good job at the moment, Jim,' thought Cheo. 'You are pissing them off!'

Jim saw the message in Cheo's eyes and continued.

"Most truly great leaders in situations as you are in, sir, want even greater stature and glory than just his guys together catching the bad guys — which we are, by the way."

Jim continued: "And that is true to the death between you, sir, as the great leader, and, well me. I am not proud to admit this at the moment, but, yes, I lead these guys — and, sadly I lead them into your capture. I am confident they want me dead."

"So, if you are the leader-warrior I believe you are, how about you and I have a, say, well, knife fight. Your knife is certainly bigger than my knife," said Jim as he carefully and slowly took his five-inch straight blade dagger out from inside his shirt.

"I do not like this situation at all, but it is my destiny, I assume, to fight you knowing all along I will eventually die at your hands. I will succumb to that closing of my life, but you must blindfold my people and tie their hands behind their backs and let them leave now. You need to let your men have fun too, and once I am with my God, they can catch up with these two 'whatevers' and finish everything in splendor — just like an Inca sacrificial celebration!" Jim was thinking-as-he-was-going, and he was beginning to run out of ideas.

"*Si!*" cried the Incan leader.

"*Lo haremos imediatamente!*"

Ruth and Cheo had already been prepared for the hunt and sacrifice and were standing at the door of the Bodega Central. They each could easily get out of the ropes, but they decided to let the drama play out. Cheo had his secret .45 Smith & Wesson ready.

Under the watchful eyes of the three hoodlums with rifles, Jim began to prepare for his final battle.

The Incan warrior leader was always ready. He just dropped what he had in his hands at the time, and gracefully withdrew his manchette-knife combination weapon out of its beautifully embroidered leather sheath.

Suddenly, Jim pulled a small piece of paper out of his pants pocket and acted frustrated that he had done all this preparation for self-sacrifice and had failed to share some additional information with the other five individuals in the room.

Just before Jim was about to speak, he pulled out his obviously well-cared for and often used five-inch dagger — sharp on both sides — and laid it on the table to his right.

"Aye!" Jim stated. "I forgot to read you a message prepared for you, and other powers out there like you, before I am authorized to participate in any duel to the death ... something that my government, the government of the United States of America, probably with the strongest Army and Air Force in the whole world, takes very, very seriously because of their participation in the League of Nations and the World courts."

"Let me read this quickly, and we can get this over with."

"To whom it may concern, a sincere condolences from the President of the United States of America (my boss). James Arthur Barclay (that is me) is required by the rules of law to inform you — before any duel that will endanger the lives of our enemies — that he is one of the most lethal knife fighters currently in this entire world (Jim spread his arms as if he was describing the last big fish he caught). He was taken from his mother at birth to be trained for this one purpose — to fight knife fights for the United States against enemies of the United States (I know, it just does not show, but you know …). Most sincerely, Franklin Delano Roosevelt, President of the United States of America."

By the time Jim had gotten to the 'Most sincerely …' part of the message, the four thugs had hurriedly left, and Ruth and Cheo had freed themselves. All their 'Made-in-the-United-States-of-America' paraphernalia had also been left on the table.

"Oh my, Jim," stated Ruth in relief, and some disgust. "Your best sermon yet, Preacher!"

Cheo, who was used to this type of behavior from his long-time friend Jim, issued a loud but short laugh from the gut.

"Let's get out of here before they think … or even know that they just need more men."

And they disappeared back into the jungle.

But not without one last word from Jim — "Ruth, that is the second time you slipped up and almost got us killed. I do not want to die because my smart colleague did something stupid. Think! No more!" Very stern.

Chapter 23

Maracaibo, Venezuela
July 1944

Alexis was a continuous learner. She attended numerous lectures and was a part-time student of South American studies at the Universidad (culture, language, 'political disruptions' — as her favorite teacher called revolutions — legends, and conquest).

One of Alexis's favorite legends mixed with, unfortunately, very real conquests, was the destruction by the Spanish *conquistadores* — literally the Spanish conquerors — of the incredible South American Inca empire. This is not the place to study and discuss the Incas but suffice it to say that the Incas had no match in the Western hemisphere with regard to cultural sophistication, dominant reign by royalty, networks, and communication systems, and, of course, extreme amounts of gold.

In 1533, Spanish conquistadors landed on the western shores of what is now Peru, and they were in pursuit of this gold — no holds barred. Of course, they had the sanction of Pope Clement VII and of all the politicians and high-ranking members of the Spanish catholic church elite. Following maps and descriptions of the time, Pizarro and his cronies raped and pillaged their way from the sandy coast up into the rocky Andes mountains to the capital city of the Inca empire — Cuzco. Imagine this trek up and down small hills to bigger hills, then small mountains to bigger mountains, to deep gorges and even higher mountains and thin air — all in the garb of the time, which included thin leather boots and heavy layered metal armor.

Actual gold, and legends of actual gold, have been the highways of destruction of many. Certainly, that was true for the conquistadors and the Incan empire. Rape and pillaging, along with European diseases and weapons, drove the Incas up into the Andes and down into the Amazon into distinction. The conquistadors had heard of the gold, silver, and gemstones in Cuzco, they just did not know exactly where it was. When they finally reached what they thought was El Dorado, it ended up being the beautiful city of Cuzco. There was plenty of treasure, and countless Spanish galleons and armadas were able to bring the treasure to the courts of the King and Queen of Spain, and the church. But, the treasure found ended up being much less than what was hoped for, and then over half of what was found was lost at sea traveling around the dangerous Southern tip of the South American continent, across the Atlantic Ocean, and away from the greedy hands of governmentally sanctioned, and many non-sanctioned pirates of the era. Sir Francis Drake is one such 'pirate' who comes to mind.

But even the twentieth century had and has its own looters — including an evil, world-domination focused, nationalist leader such as Adolf Hitler and his personal photographer, Hans Ertl. Hitler was quietly fascinated with the writings his minions found in Vatican archives. Yes, his minions even entered and polluted the archives in the Holy City and Church of Rome of a sixteenth-century South American catholic missionary named Andres Lopez. These documents, some of which remain in the Vatican, describe in detail a large Incan city rich in gold, silver, and gemstones located deep in the treacherous Amazonian jungles in what is now Peru, Ecuador, Venezuela, Bolivia, and Brazil. The Amazon river begins as a trickle of melting ice high in the Andes mountains, travels down through the dangerous jungles of the aforementioned countries, and empties into the Atlantic ocean in northeastern

Brazil. In addition to the length of travel, the river is home to some of the most dangerous living creatures God created — natives in the form of local and 'unfriendly' Indians, piranha, crocodiles, black panthers, snakes, spiders, tarantulas, scorpions and a few other delightfully lethal things.

Chapter 24

Maracaibo, Venezuela
July 1944

The sky was clear and dark, the humidity and heat were high, and Alexis had just finished dinner — again, alone. It was now late July, and she had kept track of how often Jim was home with her. Now twenty-five years-old, and very much separated from her prior world. Comparing the two worlds was relatively easy. At home in Connecticut, everything was crisp and clean — here, dirty and dirtier. There, you had some humid hot days in the summer — here, you had some dry days in winter. There, you could always run to the club and get away from things you had to do and watch others do work at the club for you.

Alexis's horses — Snow, Spirit, Luci, and, of course, the black stallion named Double Midnight — so, so very black. She missed regular competitive riding very much. She had been taught well, sat well in the saddle; jumping was like flight, and the medals and awards were plentiful. So were the Bible studies, time at church and church events, home devotions, and statements and direction and overview from Alexis' father to his only child who just happened to be smart, attentive, respectful, knowledgeable, and, at that time, a tad I, inquisitive.

Naïve no longer. There were other American and English families in Maracaibo. Almost all of the ladies of the homes met at least twice a month at the American Club; very stylish — English teatime.

The gossip was overflowing — from who is President Roosevelt spending time with (meaning, a woman for pleasure), to whose wife at the refineries was with whom (not her husband), etc.

Mother religiously went to these events, if for no other reason than to speak English with someone and find out what was happening in the United States. At these events Alexis was a wall flower, just observing and soaking things in, in an effort to know who each wife was, what role her husband played down here in Maracaibo, who that woman was married to, and who she was having an affair with.

The husband not being home was a common complaint, but at least most of the husbands did eventually get home every night — unlike Jim!

Alexis also participated at the American church on Sunday mornings and evenings and at the local Spanish church that Jim spent time at when he was in town. After all, we did come down here to be missionaries.

Chapter 25

Lorient, France
July 1944

The smell of oil, diesel, and exhaust fumes was heavy down in the submarine docks at the large German U-boat facility in Lorient, France. They were well underground due to the constant bombing by the English and American bombers along the French coast.

Usually, the docks were exceedingly busy — but it was 2:00 a.m. on the French coast, and only the minimum number of men required were working hard and cursing under their breath at the two German 'masterminds' at the railing above them.

"Conquering the world requires careful planning, doesn't it?" Hitler asked of Heinrich Himmler, his right-hand man.

"Yes, Mein Führer. It does. So does living well in each corner of the world."

"No jungles. No heat. No humidity, please!" delighted Hitler.

"Mein Führer. If we plan this correctly, we can just get rid of everything on earth that irritates you. Other than me, of course," smirked Himmler. Hitler ignored the bad joke. This always made the joke-teller nervous — including Himmler.

"Even the Jews?" asked Hitler kiddingly.

"That and the elimination of all other undesirables will be completed well before this war in Europe is won, Mein Führer!"

U-480 sat quietly just below the evil men. It was beautiful, sleek, and unique. In the hands of these two, it was also more than that. U-480 had just completed one of its most important missions — it sank four ships just off the Normandy coast during last June's Allied invasion of France at the Normandy coast. It happened to be in the right place at the right time. And, even with the 'evil sonar' invented by the crafty English three years earlier, neither the British, Australians, Canadians, nor Americans could find her as she obliterated tons of supplies and soldiers the Allies had counted on during the invasion.

You cannot sink what you cannot find. And you cannot find a sub that does not ping back to sonar. Sinking the enemy's ships at will was always the goal of the Germans, and they did so prior to the use of sonar and convoys. The invention of sonar had pretty much saved the convoys traveling to Europe, as they provided supplies and material to the Allies. The German 'wolfpacks' had, at least until the likes of U-480, been defanged and declawed.

But this mission would be different, and the massive undetectable ship would not be returning — at least not for a while.

"The enemy can see all our other weapons — jet planes, rockets, deadly gas — but not this! The rubber tiles covering this amazingly quiet and fast U-boat of ours is an accomplishment that our scientists can be rewarded for later. Keeping this quiet and secret has not been easy, Mein Führer," growled Himmler. "Even those who I thought were coming close to figuring this out, are no longer with us!"

No torpedoes, minimal ammunition, some food and water, and just enough room for eight men; usually, twenty-nine men were required to manage all the systems and weapons on the U-boats.

And of course, something more important than life to these two — funding for the future of the 1000-year Third Reich — gold bullion recently smelted and non-traceable from jewelry previously owned and treasured by millions of dead or soon to be dead Jews, orphans, gypsies, Poles, Russians, political prisoners, the mentally disabled, physically deformed, and other people Hitler just did not like from all around Europe — particularly Poland and France.

And there was already another U-boat just like this one that has been filled and sent out to sea on a similar mission.

"Any idea if the British have figured out the mystery yet?" asked Hitler.

"No. Very frustrated! And I have been assured they will stay that way for a very long time. Wait ... forever — they will never figure this out!" bragged Himmler.

"How many dock workers and the soldiers are here tonight?" Hitler asked.

"Everybody is at home but for the nine workers and six soldiers," Himmler responded.

"And?" Hitler asked.

"The workers will be executed immediately upon completing this load. After that, these same soldiers will have coffee with me in the worker's lounge. Unfortunately, their coffee will be poisoned — immediate death. Their families will all be on the train to Auschwitz by 8:00 a.m. tomorrow," sneered Himmler.

"Good," was Hitler's only response.

"Mein Führer, by 5:00 p.m., those who are aware of the entirety of this matter — other than you and I — will be dead."

Hitler stopped and looked right into Himmler's evil eyes. "You keep it that way."

But two Americans and one Venezuelan already knew about one of the new U-boats.

Chapter 26

Merida, Venezuela
August 1944

Alexis gasped slightly as she saw her reflection appear in the mirror. 'Some hotel mirror!' she thought. It reminded her of visiting the hall of mirrors in Versailles with her mother and father in 1935.

A fourteen-foot-high floor-to-ceiling mirror. At least equally as wide, Alexis observed.

"Here I am," she mused. Up in the higher elevations of Merida. Jonathan had planned everything, and as of this moment, everything was perfect.

And the three luscious dress selections, Jonathan — or somebody — had laid on the bed for her. Each deserving of the right to be worn by Alexis and displayed in the magnificent mirror. The shoes were equally perfect, in shades of colors that melted into the appropriate gown. All the undergarments too, Alexis whispered to herself, somewhat embarrassed. How did Jonathan get all the sizes correct? *All* the sizes, Alexis wondered.

The hotel's handmaid had placed the makeup perfectly on Alexis' perfect face. She set her hair perfectly on her perfect head. She also assisted in fitting Alexis into the perfectly fitting dress. And, throughout all this, nobody was sweating, thanks to the numerous elegant ceiling fans, and this miracle called 'air conditioning'. So, this is heaven here in Merida, Alexis thought to herself.

And there she was — dressed as if she were going to her senior prom. No, even better: dressed perfectly for the December 1, 1939, annual Governor's Ball at the club when she was twenty. President Franklin Roosevelt and his wife were to attend that year! Sadly, just three months earlier Germany did what her father said they would do — invade Poland. The President had stayed in Washington, D.C. struggling to keep the United States from sliding into another European war. Fortunately, his wife did not attend alone — as was rumored. Alexis' dad hated Germans and had killed many of them. They had killed his friends.

Regardless, Alexis had spent a wonderful evening with her father. He beamed with pride as Alexis slipped her arm into his as they stepped down the carpeted stairs into the ballroom. The large windows reflected the lights, the flowers, the candles … and Alexis. Most of the men there would sneak peeks out the same shimmering windows overlooking the club's swimming pool during the summers — Alexis had been the perfectly shaped and tanned lifeguard for the previous three summers, and these men clearly had fantasies as they looked at her wet bathing suit, with her skin shimmering in the sun. However, now she was not a tan sexy young lady in a perfectly fitting bathing suit — but she did now look sophisticated yet sultry, worldly yet innocent. Certainly she continued to let her memory slip back to being the young woman in an evening gown accompanying her handsome and stately WWI hero father at the club (mother truly did not enjoy President Roosevelt's "overbearing and manly wife", as mother referred to her, so she stayed home).

She again looked into today's mirror, no longer innocent, mother thought of herself with feigned disgust, now more worldly.

Here in Maracaibo, with a German major on the way to meet her. Jonathan would ring the suite's doorbell in about twenty minutes. Alexis was ready … all of her, except her conscience and her wedding ring. No matter how perfect she looked, she was not the perfect Christian missionary's wife ... and, to make matters worse, she was going to spend time with Germans! What would Jim and her father say?

Alexis quickly slipped off her wedding ring and placed it in the small table drawer. She took the time to memorize which table and which drawer, just as Jim had taught her when he warned her to always stay alert, know where she was, and memorize your surroundings. They turned this into a game they would play at least twice a week. Jim would approach Alexis from behind and say: "Alexis! Look behind you!" Alexis was required to turn and look for two seconds, turn back around, and tell Jim three things she had observed. Later, it became seven things. She challenged herself to beat Jim, which to date she had not. Amazingly, and thanks to this game, neither Jim nor Alexis ever misplaced an item.

The doorbell rang once.

Alexis took one last look at her entire self and picked up her silver clutch and the matching Hermes scarf. She took a deep breath, which made her breasts show a little more than she intended, she noticed.

She opened the door smoothly. And there was the impeccably dressed and handsome German Major. "German," Alexis said to herself again.

He stood in the doorway, just looking at Alexis for what seemed an eternity.

"As I expected ... and anticipated," he said softly. "Magnificent beauty."

For a moment, Alexis felt extremely happy and self-assured. She had not had a chance to be this 'magnificent beauty' for quite some time, and here was a man who obviously appreciated it.

He also needed it, which is another feeling Alexis had not felt for an even longer time.

"The men at our table will be envious of me. The women at the table will be jealous of your beauty. How wonderful," Jonathan quietly exclaimed to Alexis.

"Even more so now," said Jonathan as he opened the small black felt box he took out of his right inside coat pocket.

There was a dark red ruby, at least two-carat, in the middle of a webbed yet quite thin gold chain.

"Jonathan!" Alexis gently exclaimed to the Major as she slowly turned around and raised her hair lying on the back of her kissable neck. "Borrowed," Jonathan stated firmly.

"Not tonight," Alexis answered without skipping a beat.

"Oh." Jonathan answered.

"This will work", Jonathan said as he offered his hand to Alexis. The door closed as she left the room.

"Oh, my key!" Alexis said urgently as the door locked.

"I have one myself," said Jonathan continuing to look straight down the hall.

"Oh really!" Alexis' mind exclaimed loudly.

Jonathan did not hear her, of course, nor did Alexis's cadence waiver in the least as together Alexis and the Major walked away from the perfect hotel room toward the perfectly decorated elevator at the end of the perfectly elegant hallway.

'This is perfect … But it isn't,' Alexis thought.

Perfect, but for the wrong reason.

As Alexis and the Major approached the main ballroom, a servant stretched out his hand. Their eyes never met, but the Major handed over a small envelope and then slowed his pace. Alexis gracefully followed the Major's lead in everything he did. This violated her principles while away from formal occasions, but you would not know it.

Alexis was either used to it (which she was) or she just did not notice it. Either way, the same thing happened, as always. Although the small orchestra kept the same volume, it seemed like it got softer. What did happen, however, was that as Alexis and the Major slowly entered the ballroom, everybody looked. Everybody, including the servers. The couple's presence was then announced as the servant read the note from the Major aloud.

"Major Jonathan Speer and honorable guest Miss Alphonsine (Alexis) Saint-Omer."

'He forgot to tell her!' — the Major realized as he nervously pulled on his shirt collar. He gently squeezed Alexis' gloved hand and she got the message immediately. The famously mysterious and sophisticated French House of Saint-Omer. Thirteenth-century French heritage and aristocracy, known for their world travels. "Act like it!" Alexis said to herself as she quickly caught onto the theme.

He released her right hand, and she placed it on the back of his outstretched left hand. She was gliding as she walked, very much like the future Grace Kelly, but the Major, although handsome, was no Cary Grant. Alexis accompanied the Major, as one, to the line of the arrogant and pseudo-sophisticated and somewhat-aristocratic Venezuelan gentry.

"C'est un honneur pour ma famille d'etre ici avec vous et les vôtres," ("It is an honor for my family to be here with you and yours"), Alexis said gently and almost too quietly as she curtsied again and offered her hand to the large and overly dressed hostess and host. The words were right in-line with what French aristocracy declared as they entered the domain of those of similar aristocratic heritage.

The words flowed from Alexis' lips as if French was the only language she spoke, and she was indeed a long-time member of the House of Saint-Omer — and bored of having to remind someone.

"Amazing," whispered the Major to himself.

After much — too much — small talk in French, Spanish, German and English, *the* couple was led to their dinner table.

"Is it just a coincidence that my gown elegantly and subtly matches the table settings?" Alexis whispered into the Major's ear as he assisted her into the chair.

"Is there nothing you do not notice?" the Major whispered back as if irritated with Alexis.

"No!" mother responded. "Especially on a 'first date," she added with a soft and inviting smile.

"Oh really?" was all the exasperated and tongue-tied Major could say in response.

Your behavior while sitting as a couple at an orchestrated table of other couples is much like a game of chess: listen, observe, act — not react — and wait for the response. 'Easy and fun to play,' Alexis thought. She knew she was probably the best in the world at this, second only to her father. She learned from the best 'player'. She smiled, thought of a prayer blessing her father, and nodded at the other six individuals at the table.

The assumed that natural expectation — of course he must provide for his family, he is the man — and assumed societal requirement — of course we need to hire him, he has the responsibility to provide for his family — translate into more work for a woman, for her to even get to where a man begins.

'There is nothing natural in a woman's ability to impact her tributary — at least not in 1944, for goodness sakes,' Alexis thought.

But it was true. First, there is no natural expectation that she must provide for her family — oh, look, she supplements her husband's income and work — and second, there is no assumed societal requirement that a woman is to be the provider — oh, look, her husband has great income, so it's not critical for her to also work. Thus a woman must first prove her worth to work — she must provide for her family — and second, she must associate with persons who hire her individually — I do not care what her husband makes, we pay and promote her on her merits.

"Alexis!" whispered the Major sternly in Alexis' left ear.

"Oh, I am so sorry," she responded to the other six at the table. "I need to drink more water. Feeling a little light-headed at-the-moment."

So, who were the other six — or, better said, the other three couples at the table? To Alexis' right sat a rather heavyset man in what appeared to be an Italian tailored summer suit. Certainly rich — he owned many ranches, many cattle, many rubber trees and factories throughout Venezuela and Colombia near the

Orinoco river, claimed and battled over by both countries to this day. 'Inherited wealth, I am sure,' Alexis thought. Jonathan had whispered to Alexis: "He makes ninety percent of the condoms used in South America — and ninety percent of this continent's people are Catholic!"

The heavyset man and his not so nice-looking wife, who looked like a witch from Transylvania, had their elbows on the table and ate and talked with their mouths open. Fortunately, thought Alexis, they did not talk much.

To the right of the 'witch' sat another uniformed man, either from Portugal or Brazil, because he and his 'niece' were speaking Portuguese — a language that Alexis wanted to learn, but her language repertoire was full.

"He is telling his niece that he cannot wait to get back into the hammock with her," whispered the Major.

"Hah! I knew it … and, you know Portuguese as well," she responded quietly.

"And what do you think of the couple next to me? He too is with his niece!" the Major delicately stated.

Alexis acted a little surprised. But, of course, most successful men in South America had a so-called mistress — it was expected, and the wife generally knew all about it.

"Do not ask me if I am surprised," Alexis said in a judgmental way, not even thinking about what the others were thinking of her. They all knew the Major was considered by many as *the* most eligible bachelor of Venezuela. "And probably every other country he went to," Alexis said under her breath.

"Sorry, Alexis, I did not understand you."

"You heard that?" Alexis questioned.

"Yes, and that is why I am sent to these miserable dinners. I hear all I need to hear … and more. I was trained that way. I can even read lips in five languages," he boasted.

Alexis just caught herself before she said: "Jim too!" And then the guilt set in, and Alexis became quiet. She listened in German as the Major turned to the young, beautiful, and sophisticated niece to his left, talking in a tone as if he knew her from years ago.

Which he did.

'No wonder he did not introduce me to her yet!' Alexis thought in a jealous rage. 'He does know her, and he is trying to figure out how to introduce her to me!'

Alexis immediately, and elegantly, excused herself from the table, and stood up before the Major could stand, which he eventually did anyway. Alexis knew better than to not wait for the Major to stand and pull out her chair, but she was about to do what Alexis does — make a statement.

In three steps Alexis was behind the niece, whispering: "Join me!" in impeccable German, of course. The niece was a little startled, but greatly impressed.

The two young and most beautiful women in the room went off to the powder room together. Each thought the other was more beautiful, and yes, they would agree that they were indeed beautiful, but the jurisdiction would be at least Venezuela (not the room), and possibly all of South America. At least that is how they walked and behaved with each other.

"Uncle Jonathan told me he had a surprise for me, and you are it!" the niece said as they walked.

"Your Uncle? I thought …."

"He did not tell you? He tends to do that … it's nothing! So sophisticated and then dumb, all at the same time. Yes, he is my uncle, and when we do things together, they think I am his mistress, and he is not even married. Never will be … at least according to him," the niece said with a laugh.

"Oh really!" Alexis said in a joking way.

"But that was before he met you at customs."

'He told her that?' Alexis thought.

"He is quite smitten by you, Alexis."

"And I by him," Alexis said. What else could she say? 'She is playing a role now for sure,' she thought 'At the moment, I do not like this.'

"Well, then, I need to get to know you better … and soon. We will meet at the Military Club this weekend for tennis. Uncle Jonathan taught me, and we are now mixed-doubles champions at the Club. Do you play?" she asked.

'Yes, you twit,' Alexis thought, as she nodded in response. 'I was born with a racket in my hand kid, and I will whoop you with one hand tied behind my back!' Alexis yelled loudly, in her head.

"Well then, good. We better get back."

'The niece was certainly likeable,' Alexis thought. 'Just a little too perfect for my taste. A lot like … me. Oh my, where am I going with all this?' Alexis questioned herself as she returned to the table, allowed the Major to pull her chair, and sat elegantly.

"Everything ok?" the Major asked in French.

Alexis placed her hand on the Major's arm and patted him reassuringly: "Yes, and let's get back to English."

After the two Cinderellas had returned, the mood at the table became more jovial.

"It is this perfect French wine?" Alexis again said under her breath, as she raised her glass again smoothly to the other military man, who turned out to be a Colonel in the Portuguese army.

"No, it's you," Jonathan whispered in her left ear. Then, he blew into her ear for fun.

"You heard that, again?" she said quietly and in wide-eyed astonishment.

Suddenly, Jonathan's mood became quiet, as he quickly turned to the real niece's father and said harshly in German: "Not here, and not now!"

The father had been talking in German with the Portuguese Colonel, something about looking for submarines and a big leap for the U-boats — and was cut off by Jonathan when he said: "And we can do it here."

'Well, *that* requires an explanation, soon!' Alexis thought. But she pretended to have not heard or even seen that little exchange, and she turned to the man in the Italian summer suit.

"And you?" Alexis asked.

"No, but I enjoy watching the women play tennis in their cute little dresses," he responded while cleaning the red wine off his lips and mustache. The witch poked him in his tummy saying: "I wish he played, and I wish I played, too."

Alexis let go a small laugh and a to-die-for smile.

"You have a beautiful smile, young lady," said the witch.

"Thank you," Alexis responded cordially. "My father says my smile is 'angelic', but he admits he has never seen an angel." Alexis laughed and again thanked the witch.

"And you and your husband make a handsome couple," Alexis lied.

And so went the superbly orchestrated dinner.

'Pretty well orchestrated by the single, yet truly well laid Major, and the married, yet a hussy, woman,' thought Alexis. She began to feel light-footed and a little tired.

"I would like to return to the room, Jonathan," Alexis whispered to Jonathan.

Jonathan slowly turned to face Alexis directly. He had one of the unused butter knives in his left hand. Leaning forward as if to whisper in Alexis's right ear, he gently pulled Alexis toward him and lifted the highly polished butter knife as if it were a delicate Belgium mirror so she could view her own beautiful and delicate face.

"Yes, 'angelic' to be sure, and devilishly charming — with an agenda perhaps?" whispered Jonathan.

Alexis was a little surprised, but very flattered.

"My agenda cannot be spoken here," Alexis whispered back, with a hint of a devilishly delicious activity.

"Then we are worthy of a gentle dance," he responded, smiling.

"Just one dance?" Alexis asked.

She had not danced for over twenty-four months — not surprising since she was a missionary's wife. Wordly activities, i. e. fun, were a 'no-no', and the wedding she had dreamed of as a child, fell far short with no dancing, frolicking, or drinking.

"Oh my," Alexis gasped.

The one-hundred-and-fifty guests, staff, and local press — press? Alexis's mind screamed at herself — ALL were focused on the only dance couple to walk onto the highly polished and very slippery dance floor.

"Just ignore everybody," Alexis could hear her father say before the competitions when she was a child, but it was Jonathan's voice.

"Yes father … uh, Jonathan," Alexis said. "Yes, Major. I am honored."

"I wish you all well," Alexis said as she gave her hand to Jonathan to rise from her chair.

"Oh dear, you are so beautiful!" exclaimed the witch. "We must shop together soon. Oh, you two make such a lovely couple!"

Alexis smiled back to everyone as the Major began to guide her to the dance floor. And a photographer's lightbulb flashed.

"Even your feet whisper," the Major said quietly. He was congratulating himself that Alexis had not seen him gesture to one of his men to eliminate the danger of a photograph — that is, take the camera, open the back near a bright lamp, and pull the film. Nobody even noticed Jonathan's command being fulfilled.

But Alexis did see and was impressed and relieved.

"Thank you, Jonathan. I am happy, I am a little drunk, I am a little overwhelmed by this evening, yet still alert enough to glide with you. It took a lot of work by my mother to teach me how to melt my mind and soul into the lead's body and motion, but I am pretty good at it."

And she was.

The orchestra had just begun to play a new Glenn Miller song, and the dance floor was ready, with the lights turned down low.

And they were a joy watch.

They glided as they walked, but they floated utterly and seamlessly over the dance floor. They could not have been more graceful.

Figure 9: Alexis and Jonathan dancing in the ballroom at the Crillion Hotel.

A perfectly dressed and handsome man — 'still a Nazi,' Alexis's mind hissed at her — and a flawlessly built and clothed young woman, each having had the highest level of social training, are a delight to witness and to utterly loath.

'Unfortunately, romantic,' Alexis thought.

Jonathan stopped both in their tracks. He firmly and gently pulled Alexis towards him and whispered in her ear: "Amazing woman!" Again he blew gently into her ear. She kind of liked that.

And the perfect couple danced perfectly together, and everyone in the room watched and agreed.

"Amazing man," Alexis whispered into the Major's ear.

Even a seasoned German soldier can get weak-kneed — and Jonathan did.

"The wonders and powers of a woman," Alexis quietly marveled at herself.

Someone was watching everything that was going on, and he was struggling to make sense of what he saw — the missionary's wife with that Nazi! What the hell! What is he after? Does he know? 'Very curious and dangerous,' thought the United States ambassador to Venezuela.

Of course, the ambassador's wife was enthralled that her husband acted as if he knew the 'couple of the hour'.

Yes, he did, and that was a complication.

Chapter 27

Merida, Venezuela
September 1944

After what seemed an eternity, the two left the ballroom and walked outside for a quick stroll. It was hot and muggy but certainly better than the body odor, cigarette, pipe, and cigar smoke that had accumulated in the ball room.

"Jonathan, that was so fun. Thank you so much for bringing me along."

"It was fun for me as well, Alexis. All the different people, different walks and views of life, the elite of the elite in Maracaibo, dare I say Venezuela ... and all the deception!" said the Major with a wicked yet sexy smile.

"Yes!!!" Alexis said with a loud hiss. She loved this game her father had always played at the Club back home. "Wait. Why did you stop the fat man from bragging about all the U-boats he knows about? You were angry!" Alexis asked.

"Sometimes I wish you only spoke English!" the Major said sternly. "Loose lips, Alexis. Too many of them here in Venezuela, and certainly in the ballroom."

"About what?" Alexis asked excitedly.

"Nothing, Alexis," said the Major, and he picked up the pace on the way back to the room.

"I will find out," teased Alexis.

"Don't!" said the Major harshly.

"Whoops," Alexis said comically, as she let go of Jonathan's hand and, turning around, headed in the other direction.

"Alexis, I am sorry," pleaded the Major, uncomfortable, as he chased her.

Alexis looked like a fairy. Her beautiful and loose outfit gently met the curves of her body. She was perfect!

Jonathan grabbed Alexis by the waist, twirled her towards him, and held her tight. Very tight!

"I wish you were mine … and I am sorry," Jonathan said, as he quickly let her go.

Alexis quickly took hold of the Major again.

"Tonight, I am," Alexis said as she looked directly into the Major's eyes.

They kissed … passionately.

Chapter 28

Merida, Venezuela
September 1944

The Major unlocked the door to Alexis's room, kissed her hand and turned to leave.

"But …," Alexis caught herself, grateful that he was stronger than she.

Alexis grabbed his elbow, kissed the tip of her fingers, and gently and somewhat passionately placed her fingers on his lips.

"Thank you, Jonathan. You are a most handsome, sophisticated, and honorable gentleman, and I am the envy of all the women in South America."

He smiled that gentle smile; his eyes were bright, he blinked, then gently pushed Alexis into the room, and pulled the door closed. He checked that the door was locked … and he left. He had a rather significant and unfamiliar pain in his groin.

Alexis twirled away from the door.

The dinner was superb both in presentation and taste. Perfect blends of every type of Venezuelan spices, meats, oils, vegetables, and fruit. It had been superb. 'And the wine! The white from France and the red from Spain… so perfectly delivered, poured, and tasting,' Alexis thought.

She had eaten delicately, but what she really wanted were second and third helpings. Why waste the Chef's art? She thought:

'If I were a man, I could talk more, eat more, boast more and without much concern embarrass myself more. So different the demands and repercussions of the sexes. Men just get away with a lot of things that women do not. Why? Because men control the tributaries of power. Meaning what, Alexis? Meaning that life is a construct of energy — the energy of everything ends up flowing into a mighty river of eternity — the river of all life. Our individual lives are tributaries that feed into this river of life. And, just like all mighty rivers — take for example the awesomely complex Orinoco that is just several hundred miles away — the larger the tributary, the greater the impact the water flowing from the tributary has on the direction and flow of the river itself. But it isn't fair! From birth, men are gifted with the 'assumed natural expectation' and 'assumed societal requirement' that they must access and can properly utilize the available tools to make their tributary productive and powerful, and possibly even stronger than the river itself (all life energy). And when the might of that tributary slams into the even greater might of the river itself there is a definite element of change that affects the river in every way. How fun and fulfilling,' Alexis thought.

Alexis had no doubt, but also no proof, that the Major had placed sentries at all entrances of the hotel, and she was the safest she had ever been, except in the arms of her hero, her father.

Alexis saw that the bath had been run, and her sleep-wear was placed carefully on the love-seat just inside the expansive bathing and dressing area.

She carefully removed her beautiful clothing and noticed that the other two selections for this evening's affair had been taken away. There was a place for the gown just inside the closet.

She slipped into the lavender-scented bathtub.

Suddenly, she dove below the water surface and stayed there for at least sixty seconds.

Surfacing, with soap suds on her head, in her ears and gently on the tip of her nose, she smiled … and then turned grim.

What would Goldie think of this?

Goldie was Alexis's 'bestest' friend. Jim and Alexis loved her, and she loved them back. She loved Jim back more, and Alexis knew it.

Anyway, what if the Major had entered my room? What if he had been able to kiss her? Would I have kissed him back?

What if he had demanded, teasingly, to kiss me? What if he had pulled me into his arms? What if he were watching me right now … no, not him. He is such a gentleman! Just like Jim.

But he is not Jim, my husband! He is Jonathan! Not my husband!

Am I becoming a whore? Am I already a whore? This is all too dreamy, well planned out, and sophisticated to be whore-like! But there are many sophisticated whores. And a whore is a whore, as mud is mud!

Is this the beginning of something? Should I make it the end of this something? Is this the middle of something? Does he really consider me that attractive? Well of course!

What is he after? — Seems like way more than making me one of his trophies — of which I am sure he has many, where Jim has absolutely none, except for me! Which is better? I cannot believe I am even asking this question. Yes, I can!

"What if I am told to kill him. Would I? Yes."

"What if I he was ordered to kill me? Would he? Yes."

Mother cut her bath short, dried off as if a person were watching, then ran and jumped on and then into her prepared bed. Wow, using blankets when it is nine billion degrees outside. Aye! Maracaibo, Venezuela. Hell on earth! Why am I here, and why am I here-here?

She fell asleep.

Chapter 29

Merida, Venezuela
Late September 1944

Upon leaving Alexis at the hotel, the Major went straight to his waiting car. There was a slight breeze —God's air conditioner — but the Major still had to wipe sweat beads off his brow.

After handing his long-time driver his uniform jacket with the swastika — "disgusting symbol," the Major whispered under his breath — Jonathan leaned back in his hot leather car seat and tried to relax his tense body — 'Yes but,' he thought, 'I serve my country.'

'This goddess is killing me!' the Major thought as he adjusted his body for the trip home.

He had never left a woman alone in a hotel room he had arranged and paid for.

'Jim's wife,' was the next thought. 'What are you doing?' he scolded himself. 'What is Jim doing? I have not seen or heard from him for three weeks, and nobody who is supposed to know Jim's every move ... knows!'

'And Alexis, a sophisticated yet natural woman ... a mystery to me.'

'What is she up to? Does Jim know she is with me? Are they really married? Can I trust Alexis? Well, hell, she certainly should not trust me. His mother had warned the Major about women.

Men loving or pretending to love women was a hereditary trait, and skill, of his aristocratic Prussian-Bavarian family for over one hundred years.'

"Yes ... but I think I am falling in love with this princess! And I should not!" the Major whispered to himself. He reminded himself that he had a job to do ... and Alexis is either part of it by design, or fate, or mistake, or ... 'she may be falling in love with me too!'

'And she misses nothing! Damn Senor Hidalgo. Yes, he is excited about the project with his rubber plant, but loose lips must be closed, maybe permanently!' thought the Major.

"What if I am told to kill her. Would I? Yes."

"What if she was ordered to kill me? Would she? Yes."

"Oh ... fubar!"

Chapter 30

Merida, Venezuela
Late September 1944

Alexis loved diamonds and Tiffany's … but not a 3 a.m. sharp with the muffled ringing of the alarm clock.

She banged around on the nightstand nearest to her, searching desperately for the cause of the cruel awakening. But, of course, as the alarm continued, she soon discovered that the clock was on the nightstand farthest from her. She jumped out from under the covers, crawled over to the other side of the bed, fumbled to turn on the light, found the 'Alarm Off' switch, and threw the clock onto the nearby couch, 'left-handed even,' she thought.

As the Tiffany's alarm clock settled gently in the couch pillows, it fell silent — its job was done.

'Who set that alarm? I, or the Major, will have a firm talk with the hotel manager! Why, I never …'

Alexis fell back hard onto her pillows.

'Where is Jim? Is he safe?' were her first thoughts.

The next thoughts were about the Major.

'Where is Jonathan? What is he up to and what are his intentions? Why does he know so much about Jim? Other than awfully great sex (she flattered herself), what does Jonathan expect and want from me? Can I trust him? What if he knows ….'

And then, remembering the fine, perfectly presented French and

Spanish wine selection at the fabulous dinner, she made an effort to fall sleep.

'But not yet,' Alexis thought. She was in love with two incredible men, two distinctively different upbringings, two different goals in this strange world, they should hate each other, but they do not … at least not yet. What will happen when Jim knows! He eventually will know … Jim is incredible that way. She needs to know when he knows. Does he know? What will she do then, and between now and then? Oh my. What a mess! Fun though…

'Am I trying to get back at Jim for being gone all the time?'

'The tables had been turned,' she thought.

"I am Barclay David, Jim is Uriah, and the Major is Uriah's wife Bathsheba," she whispered to herself. She knew the Biblical story very well — from Sunday school and through one of Jim's recent sermons.

She also reasoned, based on a crooked and disturbing twist of theology that 'yes, but Bathsheba gave birth to Solomon, the wisest of all the Kings of Israel,' following a 'yes-but-something-good-came-out-of-all-the-evil' kind of reasoning.

'With all I know, Jim knows, he knows about this!' Alexis desperately reasoned.

"Shit," a word Alexis rarely used. She would find that Jonathan used 'fubar' all the time — his only swear word others would hear coming from him.

Chapter 31

Orinoco River Mouth, Venezuela
Late September 1944

At about the same time Alexis woke up again, Jim was eight hundred miles away, thinking about how he delighted in creating explosions.

He always smiled when he remembered what his high school science teacher taught him — if you toss a lit match into a puddle of diesel fuel, the match will go out. The same is almost true of gasoline — but it is not. The difference is the vapor pressure and density of the two liquids.

Gasoline has a much higher vapor pressure, so gasoline vapor mixed in the air above it makes gasoline flammable and explosive.

Diesel has a higher density and is much less flammable than gasoline because it has a lower vapor pressure. However, once you get diesel burning, diesel creates a significantly higher thermal energy explosion, a huge explosion, when compared with gasoline.

Jim had built the perfect portable igniter to turn barrels of diesel into an inferno.

The problem was that each new explosion required another igniter! Well worth it if the ensuing explosion stopped just one U-boat, Jim had been told many times.

Even before the beginning of WWII, with the September 1, 1940, invasion of Poland by the Germans, the German navy established highly secret diesel depots around the South American continent. The great majority of these depots were placed on the coasts of the countries of Venezuela, Paraguay, Argentina, and Brazil. Surprisingly, there were none in Chile or Peru. Why? Control of the Atlantic — and the Atlantic was Germany's highway to what it needed the most to complete world domination — meant massive and unimaginable amounts of natural resources and significant number of human slaves.

And, with the over 1,600+ U-boats planned and built by Germany to control the Atlantic, fuel was everything. How do you get fuel to the U-boats who ran on high-energy and dense diesel fuel? By means of a specially constructed fuel transport submarine, of course. Code name — Milk Cow.

These Milk Cows would prowl the coastlines. They had minimal crews, not the standard twenty-nine men. Unlike their fuel counterparts, they carried no torpedoes and only one exterior 30-caliber fixed machine gun, not the standard 50-caliber. Their internal and external tanks, and the area between their outer shell and their pressure-protective skin, was filled with diesel — the life-blood for the many killer U-boats on patrol around the world (mostly the Atlantic).

At this very moment, Cheo whispered: "How much longer are you going to stare at the place? Let's get this done and run."

Jim smiled. Cheo, Jim's closest friend and champion from 1939 through 1967, was the most impulsive and impatient man he had ever known. The direct opposite of Jim, and that made them a tremendous team.

"Something is different here," Jim mumbled. He pressed the powerful sniper's gun sight tighter to his right eye. "Movement," he uttered. "There is none. Looks staged."

Usually, there were no guards at the Milk Cow fuel depots. Mostly just rusty and tightly packed fifty-five-gallon tanks full of diesel — stacked three high and four wide, side by side, for about one hundred-and-twenty-five feet. The natural overgrowth combined with superb camouflage hid the depot from the naked eye.

"Hah. There. One click to the right!"

And, as always, Jim was correct. There was a solitary thirty-something-year-old Venezuelan army private, eating something, slouching, dirty and tired, and no firearm or rifle in sight.

"No beer either? Just dirty water?"

"Alone. But not sure," Jim mumbled. "We are here for the night. Two-hour shifts, me first."

Without a word, Cheo sighed, closed his eyes, and instantly fell asleep.

Jim quickly nudged him awake!

"Cheo, your belt!"

Instinctively, Cheo opened his heavy wide belt, threw the buckle around the huge tree branch, caught it, tightened the belt once again around his waist, and fell back asleep.

"Took two seconds. And nice camo job," Jim observed. Cheo never really had to paint his face as Jim did. Jim was white but tan. Cheo was flat out tree-bark brown. Perfect for this job. Yet he insisted on ornate camo work on his face, neck, and arms; an art form handed down by his great-great-grandfather. Or was it his father? Maybe his mother and great aunt — the story was always different. This camo, however, was a consistent, effective, and beautiful art form known only to Cheo.

The billions of bugs never even touched Cheo, Jim complained to himself. But they pioneered and settled on Jim. Always. Miserable! 'Damn, hateful and meaningless creatures,' Jim thought.

"Why did God bother creating them?" Jim teased himself. Yet Jim knew that he, Cheo, and the Venezuelan Private who was about to be killed, could also be considered meaningless creatures as compared to Jim's omnipresent, all-powerful, and loving God.

"The government God placed above me, commands that I kill … so I kill. Or is it that God kills the 'creation He loves' by means of using me, another 'creation He loves' for a greater good I will never understand? Or will I someday understand? In Heaven, I assume! Theology complicates this … I kill because if I do not, I will be killed. The government above me places me here where I must kill or be killed. That's it!!!"

"Time," Jim says quietly to the lightly snoring Cheo.

Cheo woke up with a start and his right hand automatically went for his side knife. Jim calmed Cheo with a smile, tightened his own belt, and fell asleep.

Neither of these toughened men had ever fallen while sleeping in a large old tree in the dense jungles of South America. The belt was critical, and a life saver.

The small bright speck of sunlight through a large thick green leaf woke Jim up before Cheo could.

"Still looks like he is alone," Cheo whispered excitedly. Yes, excitedly, because the sooner these two complete their obligation, as Jim called it, the sooner they will be back to some semblance of comfort and be allowed a cold shower, cool clean sheets, and a cold drink of whatever.

"OK, we're out of here," Jim responded.

For two grown men to slide forty feet down a tree to a green mattress below must be a fun sight to witness. It took no time, and within two minutes they were carrying their weapons, hand signaling each other and, like two cougars which had done this together many times before, instinctively and quietly made their way to their prey and target.

The prey was killed by Cheo.

The target was quickly prepared by Jim for destruction.

"Now!!!" yelled Jim.

Each started running full-tilt — as best you can through vines, around trees, in muck or whatever — away from the target, counting … "one-dead-Nazi, two-dead-Nazis, three-dead-Nazis."

At "sixty-dead-Nazis," and no matter where they were, they stuck their fingers deep into their ears and dove down into whatever was in front of them, Jim into an old ant pile, Cheo into a small muddy stream.

But no explosion!

"Sixty-one-dead-Nazis … Ninety-two-dead-Nazis…"

Whoomph! The initial effect is the sucking away of the air, and, Kaboom! Kaboom! Kaboom! About seventy-five kabooms, one for each of the fifty-five-gallon barrels they found, sounded like two-by-two.

The explosion-related 'dead-Nazi' cadence was not perfect, but never went beyond "ninety-six-dead-Nazis" — and, fortunately, never before "eighty-nine-dead-Nazis." Explosions of the type just endured have been known to destroy ear membranes, and, sometimes, cause the brain to turn to mush.

Both men were soon back to camp and in a cool shower, having carved their path home by using their machetes for approximately five straight hot, sticky, and itchy hiking hours. In the jungle, your prior path is overgrown within twenty-four hours. Each person rotates from front to back every twenty minutes — twenty as 'chopper', and twenty as 'looker-backer', for lack of a better name.

With his head on the pillow, Jim thought of Alexis — for the first time today — smiled, said a prayer, and fell asleep.

Jim had been told by American submariners, who had once or twice witnessed this 'depot work' before or may have even watched this one, the scene in the jungle would be unique and desolate. About a two-football-field-sized brown spot within the massive green jungle where once sat seventy-five tightly sealed fifty-five-gallon barrels of diesel, …. maybe a flame or two from the always wet, damp and thick green vegetation, the heat generated was enormous — since this was diesel fuel — metal scattered everywhere, and a small shiny hand-wheel pump, used to pump diesel fuel from the many barrels to the visiting German Milk Cow at the end of the now mostly melted and broken one-foot-wide apparatus jutting about one-hundred meters out into the sea … and, there was no body left of the dead soldier who knowingly or unknowingly was working for the Nazis.

As with any raid or commando activity conducted by Jim and Cheo, the two spent countless hours studying the target's terrain, entrance and exit, potential adversaries, their nationality, language, weaponry (Jim and Cheo always practiced being able to decipher which actual weapon was aimed at them from the sound of the enemy's loading or shooting that particular weapon), experience in battle, education, leadership and, most important, willingness to die for their cause or leader. The last item was probably the most significant to a successful action. People will die, and how willing is the majority of the armed enemy willing to die in the ferocious manner quite similar to what they just saw happen to their fellow combatant?

The common ratio was that at least thirty-five to fifty percent of the adversary would drop their weapons and run or even try to give up, even if no prisoners were taken by Jim or Cheo – enemies were simply killed. The problem is, you generally do not know which ones will run, or, if they really do run, do they run far enough so they can be counted out of the game. These persons were generally fighting to live another day for the money, drugs, and peer-prestige, not any ideological matter. They were not cowards, thought Jim. They just figured their lives were worth more than their pleasures — or the awful consequences should the top boss catch them.

Jim always credited Cheo and his colleagues, including the ever-charming Ruth, Cheo's dear friend, for being able to gather most of the aforementioned information. They were dealing with their own life or death scenarios, and Jim was deadly and seriously committed to keeping all his men, and Ruth, alive and well. And it goes without saying, this team would not even carry out any such action were it not for being a critical part of the Allied effort to stop the Axis thugs and, quite literally, save the world.

Chapter 32

Orinoco River Mouth, Northeastern Venezuela
October 1944

Spooky dark. Densely humid. Swimmable misty. And no moon. Captain Dearnst was proud of his command. Only six additional mariners, the lucky number seven. However, the Captain's cold sweat on such a hot night was due to the shame he knew he would feel after this mission was over.

'In war, a man will degenerate to his lowest possible moral level,' thought the Captain. 'This happens all the time. The lucky and the not so lucky.'

"I have always been lucky!" Captain Dearnst said out loud. Nobody was on the bridge other than he, and he was the master over the destiny of six other souls.

"It will be done. But they are as German as I. Will it be as easy as shooting the Jews?"

U417 was a special U-boat. It was recently christened by Hitler himself! Of course, Himmler was always by Hitler's side.

"Himmler is just infantry and a has-been."

'But,' thought the Captain, 'they say he came up with this plan. A critical step to world domination! This South American continent will bow to Hitler … and even me! Even if Hitler's thugs only keep half of the promises, the Dearnst name will be as recognizable to historians as the name Simon Bolivar!'

"Ah, finally," Dearnst exclaimed to nobody on the bridge.

He reached into the pocket inside his leather jacket for the controller. It was a small black box with one very red button. It was there. The Captain took a deep breath and exhaled slowly.

U417 was now in the deepest water of the Orinoco River, just seventy-five yards from a dense jungle shore dotted here and there with the figure of medium-sized and also mammoth Orinoco crocodiles.

"I hate crocodiles!" the Captain spit.

The small boat he had been waiting for was two hours late. Still dark enough though.

Dearnst flashed his lantern five times, as he was told. He then waited for forty-five seconds, and the boat flashed five times back. And after fifteen seconds of those signals, the boat flashed again two times, again as Dearnst had been told the German speed boat would do, just before it very, very quietly approached U417.

The time was now for Dearnst to act as he had done in other circumstances many times before — but not like this. He continued to pretend his friends were all Jews. It made it easier for him.

He slipped over to the hatch, waved warmly at Lieutenant Schmidt, who was twelve feet below the hatch — smiling in the dim lit cabin below.

The wave from Dearnst meant the small crew could now be awakened and leave the oven others refer to as a submarine.

As Schmidt left the ladder and headed deeper inside U417, Dearnst lifted the heavy main hatch, and with every muscle he had, he gently, as opposed to the standard slam, closed the hatch from the outside. He tightened the large hatch as tightly as he could, and placed a wrench on the top so that the hatch could not be opened by anybody inside.

"Only Hitler, Himmler and I will know about the location of all this treasure!" said the proud Captain quietly. "For the Motherland — and me!!!" he said a little louder, and with pleasure.

Dearnst slid off the deck of U417 into the waiting dingy. He smiled slyly at the grim looking and extremely muscular German sailor waiting to carry Dearnst into history.

"Where were you when I needed help closing the hatch!" said Dearnst coldly and kiddingly to Mr. Personality.

As labeled by Dearnst, Mr. Personality did not smile back.

'Very grim for a man who will become richer than he ever imagined,' thought Dearnst.

The dingy was around twenty yards from the dark grey speed boat.

'No insignia on that boat,' thought the captain. 'No flag as well?' questioned Dearnst to himself.

The dingy had stopped for some reason and began to rock.

Dearnst turned back towards Mr. Personality who was now kneeling right behind Dearnst.

The rest happened within less than three seconds.

Dearnst's throat was neatly cut to the spine, and he was flipped high into the air and off the dingy. The man was dead before his body hit the water.

Dearnst hated crocodiles, but — quite clearly, the crocs loved him.

'A question of appetite for foul German flesh,' thought the killer.

When Dearnst had slid like a snake aboard the dingy, the sailor had taken the black control from Dearnst and placed it into a waterproof bubble. He had even given the bubble back to Dearnst who would cradle it the entire time in the dingy — up until Mr. Personality grabbed the bubble, slit the German's throat, and delivered the meal to the river waters, and the crocs.

As Mr. Personality climbed into the waiting boat, his partner took control of the bubble, making damn sure it did not fall into the water!

The bubble, like the night, like the boat, like the dingy, like the faces of the Americans — was gray.

'This goes into the water, we will never find it,' thought the sailor as he held the bubble tightly as well. 'Who was the genius who created this bubble thing?'

The two American's stood and took a good last look at U417.

Together, they happily pushed the only but very red button. There were six muffled "boom" sounds that took place almost simultaneously. Dearnst had done his job well — placing explosives all along the ballast tanks of the now sinking submarine.

As the two stood and looked at U417, it just rocked a little and stayed afloat.

Mr. Personality suddenly lept up and down into the air, as if coaxing a golf ball into the cup.

And then, U417 began to sink slowly, very slowly.

The Americans could not have cared less for a crocodile's dinner nor the six souls fighting for their lives to escape their metal tomb covered in rubber. The Germans knew their effort were useless. They had been betrayed. The six would soon breath in their last breaths of oxygen-filled air, faint, and die.

The smaller American went to the wheel and turned on the engine. He kissed the small gold cross that was on the chain around his neck.

Mr. Personality took one last look to be sure U417 was gone. He confirmed the depth of the water, took his coordinates as best he could through the low mist but starlit sky. He noticed the blood still on his hands, and carefully rinsed his hands in the water — piranha were his concern for that short moment.

He took the Star of David from around his neck and rubbed it on his forehead — and then on the nine digits Hitler's henchmen had painfully inscribed on his left arm. Killing Nazis was what he did. They had tried to kill him by sending him as a little boy to Auschwitz. Incoming prisoners were assigned a camp serial number which was sewn to their prison uniforms. Only those prisoners selected for work were issued serial numbers; those sent directly to the gas chambers were not registered and received no

Figure 10: U417 going down slowly in the distance after the two Americans in the boat in the foreground triggered the explosives planted by Dearnst.

tattoos. Initially, the SS authorities marked prisoners who were in the infirmary or who were to be executed with their camp serial number across the chest with indelible ink. As prisoners were executed or died in other ways, their clothing bearing the camp serial number was removed. Given the mortality rate at the camp and practice of removing clothing, there was no way to identify the bodies after the clothing had been removed. Hence, the SS authorities introduced the practice of tattooing in order to identify the bodies of registered prisoners who had died.

This brave man with the Star of David once told Jim: "My number is 65,615. See my left arm? I escaped. My parents, brothers and sisters were immediately gassed on arrival. Only those who could work received the tattoos." At the time, Jim just sat there and cried. Hearing this also made Jim's job a lot easier on his conscience.

"We just saved this land and its people," the Jewish sailor said rather profoundly to his partner.

"Yup, we did it again. That makes two subs," returned the other as the boat sped up and took a course down the middle of the very wide river.

"Jim really knew what was going to happen — when and where. Just like last time," yelled the sailor.

"Any more of these coming?" questioned the Jewish warrior.

"I do not know," was the answer.

U417 had been filled to the gills, so to speak, with recently smelted gold bars made of gold items taken — stolen — from Jewish citizens of Poland, France, and Germany. The gold was to be used to provide initial financing of Germany's efforts to conquer the entire South American continent — beginning in Venezuela, which had all the minerals and oil to build and run all the tanks and airplanes that the Axis and Allied powers had around the world at that moment.

Chapter 33

Maracaibo, Venezuela
Early November 1944

Alexis had hit on something that made the Major squirm.

Rubber! Alexis's eyes twinkled. Her father had taught her to always ask 'why'. And she did. Why did the Major stop the conversation between the Portuguese General and the German ambassador? Because he did not want Alexis to know what Jim should not know.

In the late 1800s, the English empire played a key role in taking massive amounts of rubber tree seeds from the jungles of Colombia, Peru, and Brazil back to London. There the seeds were germinated and sent off to the Empire's South Pacific islands, and massive rubber plantations were developed.

At times such as these, Alexis would sit at her table in the kitchen, and start a bullet-point session with herself. She already knew that rubber trees are native to the rainforests of the Amazon and Orinoco basins, and the trees grow quickly. What makes rubber trees so special is the milky substance that emerges from them whenever their inner bark is cut into or damaged. It is this pure white latex that is the source of natural rubber.

Now she began one of her personal benefit bullet-point sessions, as taught to her by her father as a method to fully reason an issue. The session resulted in the following:

- *History has proven that no country can plan on winning a basic world war without access to critical wartime resources — generally, oil, rubber, and minerals to make metal.*
- *Prior to the turn into the twentieth century, South America, and here mostly the Orinoco region, was the world's most prolific source of latex from rubber trees. The trees are 'milked', similar to tapping for maple syrup.*
- *The need for rubber for many day-to-day home and military products caused a boom in demand even before the 1900s. Portugal and Spain controlled much of South America, and of course, other countries paid significant fees to grow and harvest rubber trees in the jungle. The British decided to purchase Hevea brasiliensis seeds from successful plantations in the Amazon and Orinoco basins, and they created huge rubber tree plantations in South East Asia which allowed them to control more than eighty percent of the natural-rubber market. The South American rubber industry collapsed.*
- *In the late 1800s, the English empire played a key role in taking massive amounts of Amazonian rubber tree seeds from the jungles of Colombia, Peru and Brazil back to London. Here, the seeds were germinated and sent off to the Empire's South Pacific islands, and massive rubber plantations were developed.*
- *In 1941, shortly after Japan's surprise attack on Pearl Harbor, Japan invaded Southeast Asia and Indonesia for many reasons, but none greater than their military's need for oil and rubber.*
- *Once Japan controlled the Pacific islands by early 1942, they also controlled almost one hundred percent of the natural-rubber production, and exports to Europe and the United States ended.*
- *When World War II was in full swing, the British and Americans blockaded any exports that were headed to the other two Axis Powers — i.e. Italy and Germany.*

- *Germany and Italy had stockpiled rubber imports before World War II. But it was not enough. When Hitler took control of Germany in 1933, he began preparing for war. He subsidized the development of synthetic rubber, and by 1943, synthetic rubber accounted for over ninety percent of Germany's rubber supply. However, nothing was as strong, reliable, and flexible as natural rubber — and the lack of access to natural rubber held up several German and Italian military projects.*
- *And, one of those critical military projects must have to do with improvements to German U-boats. What is the issue with existing German U-boats that the Germans need rubber?*
- *What is wrong with the U-boats?*
- *??????????*
- *Need Jim!!!! Where is he????!!!! I need him now!!*

And that was it for the time.

So, that is another reason why Germany and Italy had such deep interest in controlling South America. The continent was untapped, and rich in every mineral — iron ore, gold, silver, copper, gems, vegetables, and oil — it would take to dominate the world. It also had a large, subservient working force — i.e. slaves. If the Spanish could enslave the Latin and South American peoples, so could the Nazis in 1943.

Now, things were beginning to make sense to Alexis. War materials, rubber, planes, ships, U-boats, and a population to harvest and build what was necessary. She assumed there were many parts for everything that would be made of rubber, and Germany and Italy certainly needed it.

And yet, everybody knew that Germany was already using synthetic rubber that its scientists had created. Maybe they cannot make enough? Or, nothing is as good as the real thing. Pure rubber must be better for some things. Like what? And what is the importance of rubber to U-boats? Ah, rubber could be some sort of buffer from impact of bombs or depth charges. There must be more to this...

'I need to think this through more. I am missing something,' she thought.

Alexis immediately went to her closet and pulled out a small box labeled 'Mother Hart's Things'. Alexis opened the box and quickly dumped out the hair bands, various lady's things from her mother, hair pins, some embroidery, and a few $5 gold coins her mother had deliberately failed to return to the U.S. Mint as ordered by the government. Once the box was empty, Alexis located a very small pull cord and lifted up the false bottom.

There were two things there of importance. The first was Alexis' personal pistol, a Russian Nagant M1895.

How she longed for the days she would go out into the woods on her parent's property, and with her father practice shooting an assortment of rifles and pistols. Roy knew them all and would often show off to Alexis how he could disassemble and reassemble the rifles and pistols without opening his eyes. Eventually the ever-competitive Alexis would do the same, only faster.

Ever since 1937 Alexis could hear the lecture from her father when he gave her the coveted Russian Nagant. It was a complex gun but shot smoothly and more quietly than other similar guns. Alexis suggested to her father that a silencer would make the pistol so quiet that no deer or wild turkey would be scared away should she miss on her first try — yes, few hunted with a pistol, but Roy and Alexis did.

Nevertheless, it is here that Roy would begin his lecture.

"Now, Alexis, no matter how much you want it to, a silencer does not make a gun silent. Any more than a car muffler makes a car silent. It simply reduces the noise to a more tolerable level.

How well silencers do that depends on a number of factors. The first is the actual blast produced by the high-pressure burning gases as they exit the barrel. This is what a silencer is designed to reduce.

But if the bullet exceeds the speed of sound as it exits the barrel, and most do, it produces a sharp 'crack'. This is the sonic shock wave or sonic boom of the bullet going faster than the speed of sound. This can be louder than the blast and silencers do nothing to reduce it. For a silencer to be truly effective you have to use ammunition designed to be subsonic in a given gun.

And then we come to revolvers which have another source of noise. In most revolvers, there is a small gap between the front of the cylinder and the barrel. Hot gas escapes at very high pressure creating substantial blast noise. This is why most revolvers are louder than an equivalent automatic. Of course, this high-pressure gas never makes it to the silencer, which explains why silencers are less effective with most revolvers. A silencer still reduces the sound. Just not as well.

Note that there are revolver designs that seal the gap between the cylinder and the barrel and this Nagant M1895 is one of those revolvers that I Roy gave Alexis. It requires special ammunition where the bullet is actually seated all the way into the case, leaving part of the case extending out past the bullet and here Roy would go to great lengths comparing bullets. When the trigger is pulled the cylinder slides forward and pushes the extended case neck into the barrel. This seals the gap when it fires. It works great, although it has a heavy trigger pull, about twenty pounds. So, here is the silencer Alexis wanted, and this Nagant is the only pistol Roy knew of that does the best to quiet down the noise of the escaping gas from the bullet.

Alexis knew the lecture by heart, primarily because that is what Roy wanted, and secondly, she would use the lecture to go into the card room at Roy's country club and make loving fun of her father, which Roy enjoyed, and the other cardplayers tolerated. Plus, Alexis was, in the words of many of these other card players, "very cute," and as she grew older, the compliment changed to "very sexy," and was only whispered outside of Roy's earshot.

The second item was the code book, a sharp light lead pencil, and the correct type of paper, which was not sold in your local store. Using the code for this month, Alexis wrote down the following short message: "Why would a U-boat need even more rubber than it has at production? What is it about this U-boat that it would benefit from more rubber? What are the weak points of a U-boat that the Allies would focus on? Give all reasons or answers available. Quickly."

Alexis would take this little communication to the U.S. Embassy tomorrow. She would have an answer delivered to her tomorrow evening, at exactly 8:30 p.m. Venezuela time. Black Buick sedan, no whitewalls, the driver is Korean, and Alexis knew the proper phrases in Korean to confirm.

She then packed up Mother Hart's things and placed the box once again in the back of the closet.

Chapter 34

Maracaibo, Venezuela
November 1944

"I guess I wonder why at dinner in Merida, you stopped your two friends, the Portuguese General and the Ambassador, mid-sentence — something like 'not here, not now'?"

Out of nowhere, here comes Alexis with a question that the Major had hoped Alexis had missed — but she never does. Never. Regrettably, he thought. 'Fubar.'

"I felt badly that I did that," the Major responded. "I always think the others talk too much about silly things. That is not me."

"You are correct. That is not you. It is also not you to lie to me. Just say you cannot tell me. But, never, ever lie to me, Jonathan. Again, never, ever."

"But … and I cannot tell you now," responded the Major, nervously. He had never dealt with a woman such as Alexis — and that is what was so exciting, different, and dangerous, thought Jonathan.

"What are your plans after you get home from here, Alexis? Of course, the driver will take you anywhere you need to go, as always. I have some meetings at our embassy, and then a short trip for a few days. Just here in Venezuela," the Major summarized quietly.

Alexis kept her head down, eating the banana crepe, the eggs-over-hard, the awesome fresh mango slices, and, of course, sipping black coffee, made from beans truly roasted in the sun on large concrete slabs placed where the jungle ended and the crisp but dry mountain air began, up in the Venezuelan Andes.

"Very nice of you to stop by and have breakfast with me this morning, Jonathan. I want to thank you for the elegant event last evening, the finest wine, the perfect planning of everything for me, the gown selection, the dreamy bed and sheets, the perfect bath, and, for being more than the perfect gentleman," said Alexis as she lightly touched and rubbed Jonathan's perfectly manicured left hand.

'Truly,' thought Jonathan, 'for the first time with a lovely young woman — single, engaged or married — he did not spend the entire evening anticipating gentle, hard, dominant, submissive, extraordinary love making most of the night. Alexis was not easily impressed,' he continued to himself. 'Never had that either. Not aloof, not lost, just … perfectly perfect.' Oh my, he wanted Alexis for himself so badly. 'This is complex,' he ended before Alexis spoke up.

"This is complex, Jonathan. We need to talk about all this … now. Not only am I an American fraternizing with a German military officer during a time our countries are at war with each other — and dare I say, with a German officer who appears to know more about my husband, another American, than I do. And then, of course, there is my father, who was several times almost killed twenty-five years ago while fighting your countrymen — but he killed them — in this perpetual war. Oh my, this may be one thing he would never forgive me for."

"And then," Alexis continued as if without another breath, "there are my religious beliefs, my ethical standards, my pledge of allegiance to my country and its flag, my marriage vows, my love for Jim and, you love him too, and he loves you, and …, and, my growing deep and well-thought-through affection and need for you, your company, your understanding of who I am deep down inside, your care for the smallest detail, your sophistication, and a worldly wisdom that seems to guide you, and therefore me, ... to a path and destination we may even want — but nobody in my deeply patriotic, East Coast, and conservative Christian family will want for me, and, dare I say, your equally patriotic, Prussian and Bavarian family will want for you..." Alexis stopped, gently turned Jonathan's head directly toward her, held his face tenderly, and looked very and extremely deeply into Jonathan's bluest of eyes.

"You, Major, have complete domination of my heart ... but Jim has command of the same heart. The most unique of circumstances for us. What we are doing is wrong as we know it and as defined by all who we know ... but," and Alexis paused, tweaked the Major's cheeks, held his hands together and kissed them as a Connecticut beauty's tear fell on each of their thumbs. "I would not change what has happened and I will not stop what will happen ... and, what happens is what happens. We each will compromise our standards to assure we appear to, but do not, meet the standards demanded by our God and our countries, and those who know and respect us. You know we have to do that, Major! I know you can, but are you really willing to do that, Jonathan?"

Jonathan sat silently for what seemed an eternity. As he always did, he folded his napkin, adjusted his collar, stood up, and reached out for Alexis to join him.

Alexis brushed off her face with a napkin, extended her hands toward Jonathan, and he tenderly pulled her up, extended his arms as if preparing to lead Alexis in a slow dance, kissed Alexis's forehead, led her into a pseudo slow dance move, held her very close to him, placed his mouth close to Alexis's left ear, took a deep breath, and ..... firmly and clearly whispered "the answer is 'yes', my precious Alexis, I am more than willing."

Alexis, as a wife, at this moment, felt dreadful, and as-one-of-two-who-were-once-one, disconnected from her husband Jim; and, as another's wife, at the same moment, felt wonderful, and as-one-of-two-who-are-now-one, connected to her lover Jonathan.

However, she fully and thoughtfully loved both equally now.

But Jonathan never answered why he interrupted the two men at dinner last night. He won this round of our tussle, Alexis reasoned.

Chapter 35

Maracaibo, Venezuela
November 1944

It was dark, and there was almost a cool breeze coming from the dirty Lake Maracaibo when the Nazi Officer and his princess-like friend exited the stuffy Maracaibo Opera House. "This opera house, inside and out, rivals the architecture, beauty, opulence and acoustics of some of the best in Europe," said Alexis as she put her arm into Jonathan's.

"Any more adjectives?" teased the Major.

"Maybe, Jonathan-like," Alexis shot back.

The driver had the car all-ready at the bottom of the thirty-one steps down, and Jonathan assisted Alexis into the right-side bench seat in the back. She had told Jonathan, and by now he was well trained, that she hated having to scoot across the hot leather back seat in her gown. It was difficult, stained her undergarments, and ruined her desire for any activities later in the evening. The last reason was enough for the Major. So, as always, he walked around the car to the other side — even the one time it rained, and it does not rain often in this part of Venezuela.

"The dictator of this fine country played the guilt game with the oil companies and the United States' government, reminding all that these parties would be a much less wealthy should they not fund some cultural and athletic facilities in downtown," Jonathan replied.

The city with all its lights looked magical to the 'princess', and the lights intermittently lit the driver's side mirror enough to allow Alexis to quickly adjust her hair. As their car turned right after leaving the Opera House, Alexis was fixing her hair using the left driver's mirror, and she noticed that another car, with maybe three persons, turned on its lights and did a smooth U-turn starting from the other side of the road. Turning on the lights was a catalyst to suspicion. Alexis continued to monitor the situation while Jonathan leaned forward and chatted with his driver. She also reached for the floor near her feet and adjusted the night bag she had brought with her from home — just in case.

As the couple's driver negotiated the streets to leave downtown, Alex noticed the same car making the same turns, at the same distance from them.

Alex gently pulled Jonathan back into the seat. Expecting a kiss, Alex had to adjust his head to whisper in his ear.

"Jonathan, do not turn yet, but we are being followed."

Jonathan had no doubt that Alex's judgment was correct. He smoothly reached under his seat and took out an American Colt Official Police M1917, affectionately called by its grateful users the 'Colt Commando' — a powerful, smooth double-action, and accurate .38 Special, and eighteen loose bullets. At the same moment, and tightly against Jonathan's body to assure a single glob-like figure to the outside killers, Alex lifted her Russian Nagant M1895, seven-round cylinder with its unique, and therefore considered sexy, 7.62x38mmR ammunition, and fourteen loose bullets, out of her night bag.

"Nice gun, Alexis," kidded Jonathan.

The two continued slouched-as-one as Jonathan unlocked and opened the back floor door, just as they had messed with at a picnic a few months ago.

As they raised to a sitting position, Alex used her knife to cut off the bottom part of her formal dress.

"Let's do that again tomorrow night when nobody is following and trying to kill us," whispered Jonathan. "It's kind of a damper."

When Jonathan turned to comfort Alex to tell her everything would be fine, he saw Alex professionally preparing her favorite pistol.

After a moment of looking carefully at each other, prepared to kill, Jonathan whispered: "Ok. Three in car. Two in front, one on left side back. You are on the right — you take the passenger on the back left. I am left, I will take the front driver and passenger. After you kill, roll away into the dark and stay there. I will roll left until things clear. The driver is only going to drive a half block down, stall, and pretend to try to restart. The others will approach at some point, if not right away. The first to shoot gets out of the way fast. Many families out tonight. Only one shot from you. The driver and I have practiced this many times, so we will all be fine as long as you do it correctly the first time."

"Count their shots, but assume they have plenty of ammo."

"To kill," he said finally.

"Of course, Jonathan. I have done this before, but thank you," Alexis notified her fellow combatant.

Jonathan gently kicked the driver seat once. The driver turned left on the first darker street, went to the middle of the block and feigned a stall. The car behind slowed to a stop and turned off its lights.

Alexis dropped out of the bottom of the car to the right, and Jonathan to the left. On the roll away, they winked to each other.

As the driver continued his charade, the three from behind quietly and stealthily opened their doors and began to slide out into the dark street.

At five feet away, Alex and Jonathan raised their pistols and quickly went to the front and back windows of the pursuing car. They were pros and shot in unison at the figures inside! One shot each! Alex put one shot to the head of her prey, Jonathan to the head of the front man and to the heart of the second man he had turned to run. Each of the them was dead before they fell to the ground. Two minutes later, all three of the hunters were already heading down the road at the same speed they were going when their car 'stalled'.

"Did you see the SS insignia on their right hands? Filthy SS, even if I am a German citizen," Jonathan blurted out.

"You simply amaze me with what you know and how you do it," Jonathan exclaimed relieved as he leaned hard into the back seat.

"How can you talk about sex at a time like this, Jonathan!" responded Alex in a low, sexually toned utterance.

"Huh?" answered Jonathan. He did not catch the joke.

The driver, also a pro, understood the joke, was relieved it was over, and just drove away with a smile.

'Nothing had just happened, just like all the other times with my Major,' the driver thought to himself.

Chapter 36

Caracas, Venezuela
November 1944

Jonathan and Lexi were exhausted — this more than three-hour session of sensational soul-connection and unbridled-meaningful-passion between a woman and a man was almost too much. Undeniably incredible — and new each time.

Of course, it was shower time, and Lexi was out of the bed standing under the hot steamy water a second or two after she decided that 9:15 p.m. was the perfect time for an evening walk. Six showerheads, two large hand-carved marble chairs under the falling water, and luxurious Parisian soap makes the chore of getting ready a little more bearable.

This is the time to start thinking about dinner in South America anyway; an additional consideration is that with no sun and with a cool soft breeze off the Atlantic Ocean and across Lake Maracaibo, a slow cozy walk is a must for two young romantics.

"Come on, Jonathan," Lexi whined softly to her lover. Alexis never whines. A first for the Lexi/Jonathan relationship…

Actually, the whine was perfectly cute, thought Jonathan, and he responded diligently to the call of his Delilah.

Extremely soft white Turkish sheet towels as well, and each lover dried the other in the only manner that fit that evening — gently, lovingly, and of course, seductively.

Now was the time to hurry because their favorite little restaurant on the local area plaza would stop serving around 10:45 p.m.

"I love the fountain there," said Lexi to her best friend Jonathan. "Hurry!"

Alex found her white dress, matching pumps and was ready.

Jonathan played catch-up and wore his matching pants and jacket that almost matched Lexi's clothing. He wore his brown leather-meshed sandals.

Together, the two looked happy and as one.

And they were off!

None of the neighborhood's families, couples or children paid any attention to the handsome couple approaching the old fountain. This fountain, much like every other fountain in the middle of a neighborhood in a South American city or town, ran perfectly. The water was cool and clean, and the air was hot and humid.

Alexis pulled Jonathan into the fountain!

Days later while sitting at the Club, Alexis wrote a poem about that evening:

Dancing in the Fountain
The full moon
The quiet streets
The bright stars
The fountain where we meet

The sound of the water
Falling ever so constant
Calling us to do something special
Like go dancing in the fountain

My inviting eyes immediately turn
From the passion that had begun to burn
To a signal inviting him to break the rules

Figure 11: Alex and Jonathan dancing in the fountain in a public square in Caracas, Venezuela.

Regardless of any fines we may earn
For dancing in the fountain

There is little more cool
There is little more fun
Than making waves in a shimmering pool
Moving in rhythm and ever so slowly
While dancing in the fountain

Suddenly we were quiet
Suddenly we were numb
We reached out to each other
Feeling wet and dumb

But it was then we knew
We would forever be together
Good, bad, and all in between
Will be tempered and measured by the way we felt
While dancing in the fountain

The whistles shattered the quiet
They broke the trance
There was a guard who knew
That nothing good can happen
When people dance
Where they should not
There is nothing gained
While dancing in the fountain

We grabbed our shoes
Not putting them on
There was no time
We had to be gone

So off we went
With hope to return
To the fountain in Maracaibo
Where passion and fun together did burn.

Chapter 37

Normandy, France
June 6, 1944

In early June 1944, on and around June 6, the day of the Allied invasion of Fortress Europe, four critical Allied ships were mysteriously destroyed without warning off the coast of Southern England. The destroyer knew exactly which ships to sink. How? And what was the destroyer? It was not a surface ship.

Half a century later, off the Isle of Wight in the English Channel, and fifty-five meters down, the sea revealed a WWII German submarine with a design unlike any found before. Using cutting edge investigative techniques, a team of underwater detectives discovered a story of invention and heroism, and a secret stealth technology. The submarine was identified as U-480. The investigators assume U-480 was the first U-boat to go into successful action with a special coating that made it invisible to sonar, but which could not save the submarine from a fatal trap laid by the Allies.

The most effective submarine detection device the wartime Allied Navy developed was ASDIC. It sent out pulses of sound and listens for echoes from the thick steel hull of U-boats. As the war progressed, this and other techniques meant that U-boats went from being the hunters to being the hunted, and the Germans began to lose the submarine war. To regain the upper hand, in early 1944, the Germans dispatched the very special submarine U-480 to lie in wait under the main shipping lanes that cross the English Channel. Four ships, totaling 14,000 tons, and including the Canadian warship HMCS Alberni and the British minesweeper HMS Loyalty, were sunk without warning. Apparently, only two, three, or four individuals understood how the submarine was able to make its fatal attacks completely undetected in one of the most heavily-patrolled sectors of the English Channel.

Jim, Jonathan, and Cheo knew, but nobody asked them — and they would not have said anything. The Allies, however, had a plan to deal with these new and extremely troublesome submarines. Only now do previously Top-Secret files reveal the devious traps they laid and how they enticed the Germans to fall into them. Close examination of the U-480 hull shows how she was sunk — and she went down with all hands on board.

To reduce the sonar echo of U-boats, the Germans developed sound absorbing synthetic rubber which coated the outer hull of the boats. Natural rubber worked almost four times better as a sound absorber, but it was extremely difficult for Germany or Italy to obtain during the War. Radar absorbing materials were also used to coat the snorkel heads. U-480 actually used 'Alberich' rubber which consisted of synthetic rubber sheets of about 4mm in thickness which had sound absorbing properties mixed in. The final rubbery material was named Oppanol, and it was secured to the outer hull in sheets with adhesives, much like an outer skin. Although no conclusive tests were performed, it was claimed that the echo reflection of a U-boat with Alberich was reduced by about fifteen percent — sixty percent if natural rubber with the same additional sound absorbing materials were mixed in with the original rubber latex directly from the rubber tree. The rubbery skin also acted as a sound dampener, containing the U-boat's own engine noise. Although the principle was a sound one, problems were encountered with the adhesive coat which was not strong enough to adhere the rubber sheet to the hull. This resulted in the sheets being partially washed off, which flapped in the wake of the ocean current, causing hydrodynamic resistance and noise.

Further research into more reliable adhesives was conducted, but up to the end of the war, only a few U-boats had received the rubbery skin treatment — primarily due to the intensive and laborious work it took to complete the task. The first U-boat to receive Alberich was U-11, a Type II coastal boat for trials on its sound absorbing properties. In April 1940, the first operational U-boat, U-67, a Type IXC boat which was just being laid down, was treated. Thereafter, problems with the adhesive prevented further treatments until early 1944, when U-480, a Type VII was tested again using a new adhesive and natural rubber. The results were satisfactory enough and it was decided that all new U-boats of Type XXIIIs and XXVIs would receive the coating, but ultimately only one Type XXIII, U-4709 had been completed with the coating.

It is interesting to note that submerged U-boats with or without the rubber coating employed several devices to evade allied pursuers equipped with sonar. These consisted of decoys which resembled a submerged submarine and noisemakers to blackout the pursuer's listening device. One of the most successful decoys used was the so-called BOLD canisters. The BOLD canister was a metal tube about 3.9 inches in diameter, filled with calcium hydride which gave off large quantities of gas when mixed with sea water. This canister was launched from a special tube and on release, sea water seeped into a special valve which reacted with the chemical. The valve would open and shut, causing the canister to stay at a certain depth until the compound was depleted in about twenty to twenty-five minutes.

Through use of the BOLD canister, the resulting bubble cloud would resemble a submerged U-boat to underwater locating devices such as sonar, and unless the sonar operator was especially skilled, it was often difficult to distinguish from a real target. The allies called this a Submarine Bubble Target (SBT). BOLD was widely used from 1942 onwards, with new and improved versions being developed until the end of the war. The last version was BOLD 5, and it was intended for use at depths of up to two-hundred meters.

The second most used detractor employed by the U-boats was affectionately named 'Siegmund' by the German submariners. It was an anti-sonar device which emitted a series of deafening explosions that were intended to blackout the enemy's listening gear. The U-boat would make its getaway by altering course or running at high speed during this short period.

Finally, Allies were perplexed when after the War, documents indicated there were at least three other U-boats identical to U-480 that were unaccounted for, U-317, U-490, and U-502. To date, nobody knows for sure what happened to these rubber-coated U-boats.

Again, Jim, Jonathan, and Cheo knew, but nobody asked them — and they would not have said anything anyway.

An interesting sidenote. On June 7, 1944, Jonathan point-blank asked Alexis whether she was aware of the Normandy invasion before it happened. Alex lied and said no.

Chapter 38

Caracas, Venezuela
Late June 1944

Jonathan and Alexis stood quietly facing each other in their familiar room at the Crillion Hotel in downtown Caracas. The corner suite was too quiet. Twenty-one stories up, and the street noise was music to both of them. They loved the symphony of the traffic, the horns, the sirens, the living.

The moment Alexis closed the door of Suite 2111, she locked eyes with Jonathan. He was standing at the corner window, elegant in his suit pants and cuffed white shirt. His Hermes tie, one of Alexis' favorites, was loosely hanging from under his starched collar — untied.

Alexis had arrived in her favorite white capri pants, loose silk blouse, loafers, and with her hair hanging around her exposed shoulders. He had once given her a delicate 22-carat gold locket that hung from a serpentine 22-carat gold chain and landed right between the top of her heaving breasts. That was on purpose when he selected the chain — she knew it, and he never told her.

The locket had simple but indiscernible etchings of some sort inside. If you could read it, it would still be hard to read. Small and overlapping. "Just for decoration," Jonathan had said. He should have said: "Words written in heaven telling you they miss your beauty." That would have been the clever and quietly flirtatious

Jonathan she knew. It raised questions, but not looking for answers then — unlike now.

Jonathan did not move.

Alexis, however, did.

They still looked deeply in each other's eyes.

Alexis clicked off all the lights with one movement to the two switches on the wall. She had done that before in the same room, for fun then — not now.

The city lights and sounds filled the room. And that was all.

Alexis walked within five feet of Jonathan — eyes locked. For eternity maybe, Alexis thought.

Slowly, very slowly, Alexis began unbuttoning her blouse. Five buttons, sixty seconds each.

Five minutes later, Alexis's lightly crafted silk bra laid between them. And yet, he did not move. Not an inch, and his arms remained gently at his sides. Her eyes remained fixed on his, but she could now see his heart. And, if she knew Jonathan, he now saw hers.

She left the necklace on.

Alexis then followed the same ceremony with her slacks, and panties. Her loafers remained on, for a reason.

She now stood tall, confidently, lovingly, mysteriously, defenselessly before Jonathan.

Jonathan did not move, did not smile, did not sweat — but Alexis was certain he was now hard.

Still facing each other, Alexis finally uttered a word.

"Now!" she said firmly.

Jonathan instantly obeyed. He now began his own ceremony — identical to Alexis' — but more buttons!

Now, naked together, Alexis slowly approached Jonathan. She reached down, held his firmness with her right hand, and pulled him towards the bed.

"Why the shoes?" Jonathan asked as they both fell onto the bed.

"Should I want to still run from you," Alexis quickly and laughingly replied.

"No longer," she whispered in his ear, followed by her tongue.

As Jonathan slept, Alex heard and found more information about the upcoming rubber transport.

Chapter 39

Maracaibo, Venezuela
July 1944

'Life is too complicated,' Jim thought as the plane was about to land in Maracaibo. The plane was a DC 3 with a loud, non-pressurized cabin that featured little oxygen hoses for each passenger to hold under their noses when the plane had to periodically fly higher than five thousand feet above sea level. As always, the flight attendants were each beautiful in their crisp uniforms, and the drinks and food were particularly terrific. They also spoke English, French, and Spanish.

"Hah," whispered Jim to himself. "But they do not speak German — yet!"

Jim had narrowed the purpose of his many missions for the OSS to prevent German from being a required language for flight attendants on planes flying into and out of South America. It made him laugh at himself and smile.

He was anxious to see Alexis — very anxious. He had been away from Alexis's inviting and clear eyes, perfect body, mind, and spirit for almost four months. There had been very little communication between Alexis and Jim since he left Maracaibo months ago. Why? Just because. There were only two ways to communicate between an OSS operative and a citizen spouse — and neither was particularly confidential. The first was by code from an American Embassy near

Jim at the time, to the American Embassy near Alexis. The message would be typed into English and hand delivered to the recipient spouse.

The second method was a direct phone call (if the spouse had a telephone) from the Vice President of the United States, informing the spouse that the OSS spouse had been "killed in action" or was "missing in action." Either way, the body would never be delivered home.

And then, there were those few times when Jim broke the rules and would send a message to Alexis through Jonathan, and he would sometimes receive a message back from Alexis — through Jonathan.

"Heck. She does not even know I am returning today. Should I call from the airport and tell her — warn her — that I am only 20 minutes away?" Jim questioned himself. Alexis had told Jim she did not like being surprised that way — unless, of course, there was what was called "a consequential gift" with him. "Consequential gifts" included, but were not limited to, a Louis Vuitton or Channel purse (if he was coming from Europe, or any capital city in South America), or rough diamonds or emeralds found while traveling in the virgin jungles or along the mountain streams near the small mining towns scattered here and there in Jim's travels.

Jim reached into the side pocket of his brief case to assure himself that the diamond was safely there. Of course, it was. He had picked it up just shy of the waterline in an estuary of the Orinoco. This was not an uncommon event, and more often than not the diamonds were of poor quality. However, Jim felt that there was something special about this 'rock'.

Jim's face was anxious but stern, deep in thought. He was always allowed to walk right through customs, and his friends there would wave and give a thumbs-up. Jim thought that they had some idea that Jim was important, primarily because some US embassy official from Caracas had paid the customs managers very well indeed. Of course, when Jonathan came through customs, he was treated even better — probably because the Germans threatened to kill the families of customs officials if there were any problem.

'We bribe, they kill,' thought Jim. 'Technically, which is the greater sin, or are they all treated the same?'

Alexis was not the only member of the family struggling with the concept of sin, when balanced with, or attempted to be balanced against, the greater good. It seemed that each situation demanded a different degree of sin — or did it?

'Got it!' thought Jim. 'Are there situations where even God takes into account the fact that the sin reluctantly committed (a compromise of morality) results in the only good or the greater good of another person, another person's family, or all of humanity? Does the situation ever justify a compromise of ethics? Is morality a degree higher than ethics, or are they the same thing?'

The bottom-line question is two-fold. Can you compromise somebody's ethics for good? Yes. Can you compromise somebody's morality for good? Probably not for Jim's good, at least in Jim's mind. He had indeed compromised his ethics many times to accomplish the results required of him by his government. So, when he killed his country's enemy, at his government's order, ethically he was in a sound position. Morally, however, he believed he had clearly broken the Sixth Commandment 'Thou shalt not kill,' and he would have to live with that until Judgment Day. The same with the Seventh Commandment 'Thou shalt not commit adultery.' And, of course, the remaining eight commandments came to Jim's mind as well; all because of his responsibilities as an OSS agent for the United States of America — In God We Trust.

Jim went to the waiting Venezuelan military car, climbed in (he had no bags) and requested stopping at the florist shop and then home.

'Well, there you are, Jim — you are the Baptist beacon of situation ethics. The lies, deception and killing required of him may or may not be accepted in Heaven on Judgment Day. But he had no choice. There would be no christianity if the Axis powers took over the world. But his God would take care of everything anyway. So why was he put into this situation by God anyway? Does the advent of 'the situation justifies the means' strengthen or weaken the foundational core of Christianity?' Jim would always have these thoughts — his entire life. He never felt he was ever forgiven for some things he did during his service to his country. Of course, he never felt rewarded either. I am certain that when dad had his last heart attack in 1994, and when he was conscious for a short time, he still was not sure how things would be when he arrived somewhere after death. His life history deeply troubled him.

Jim's final thought on the matter today was 'time will tell.' Certainly, a quip of an answer, but that was for another day.

Back to Alexis. He thought again of his angel here on earth. So close, yet the four months will probably require at least four days of reacquaintance, in and out of bed.

And then there was Jonathan. Handsome, smooth, sophisticated; worldly wise Prussian officer Jonathan. Alexis certainly is lonely. She may be able to fight off Jonathan's inevitable advances, or maybe she is too tired and lonely to fight off anything. Maybe she could be the advancer. Would Alexis ever advance to a situation where her loneliness, her situation, would justify her taking comfort in Jonathan or any other upper-class gentleman in Maracaibo who only need to see her to want to conquer her?

'Slow down, Jim. We are headed home. Whatever! Really? Things may have or will happen with Alexis. I'm not stupid.'

Jim put his head back and fell asleep for the remaining twenty minutes in the horridly humid and hot car.

Chapter 40

Maracaibo, Venezuela
July 1944

'Jim is not stupid …' thought Alexis as she made the final touches around the small and always dusty and hot Barclay residence in Maracaibo, '…or is it that he is too trusting?'

Jonathan had informed Alexis that Jim was coming home that day. Jonathan would never say how he knew. Did Jim know that Jonathan knew, and that Alexis knew Jim was coming home because Jonathan knew? 'Ouch!' she thought.

Alexis was sure Jim would pick up on something. She was so sure that she had decided to not even try in advance to calculate her responses should Jim start asking questions or sense something was wrong. Will the fact that she loved them both minimize the potentially obvious awkwardness if discussions turned to Alexis's activities or to Jonathan? Jim had asked Jonathan to keep an eye on Alexis, and Jonathan certainly had done that. Jim sent messages to Alexis through Jonathan, and Alexis sent messages back to Jim through Jonathan.

Do men from Jim's group, U.S. agents, know everything Alexis is doing, and do they tell Jim? Why wouldn't they tell Jim? Or, to not lose him, why *would* they tell Jim?

"Oh, the web we weave," her mother would tell Alexis when her daughter started bending the truth as a child.

Here in Maracaibo, here at this time in world history, everybody is bending the truth for their cause.

'Most of those who are deemed trustworthy are not so. I will be lying to Jim (either by omission or commission), and he will be doing the same to me. Jim will lie to Jonathan, and Jonathan will lie right back to Jim. Jim's men will monitor Jonathan's men, and vice versa. What happened to our being missionaries, to the hordes of people here who need what we have to 'sell'. What happened to our convictions?'

'That's easy,' thought Alexis. 'In the order of priorities, when we met, God was first in our lives. We were going to save the unsaved. We were going to bring light where there is darkness. Then the Feds hunted Jim down, and convinced Jim that it most certainly was God's will at this time to put country first, and then God, and then family. Actually, they convinced Jim that putting country first was putting God first — kind of like a gentlemen's tie. Now the priorities were God, God, and Alexis, in that order.

And, of course, Alexis was informed that she must monitor Jim and his behavior. She was trained to do this without Jim knowing. Now Alexis lies daily to Jim, again by commission or omission, while Jim lies back to Alexis, again by commission or omission. Effectively, Alexis's priorities were now God and God, as a tie, and Jim and Jonathan, as a tie. Whoa!'

Jim's ride just pulled up to the house.

Chapter 41

Maracaibo, Venezuela
July 1944

"Jim's home!" yelled Jim excitedly as he entered the front door.

"Yes, he is," Alexis responded as she turned the corner from the kitchen.

The two began towards each other, and together they just stopped — five feet apart.

"I have missed my angel. That is you, Lexi!"

"And I have missed my partner," Alexis responded.

"A lot," they responded almost in unison.

"How are you, Alexis?" Jim asked with the sincerity of a man who just saved his little girl from drowning.

"How are you, Jim?" Alexis asked Jim with the sincerity of a mother who just saved her little son from falling.

They immediately fell into each other's arms. They kissed passionately. Jim's hands were all over Alexis's body, as if he were checking to see if everything was still there.

Alexis accommodated Jim's moves, and immediately felt Jim's hardness even getting harder.

"I heard that when soldiers come home to their wives, all they want to do is …" Alexis teased.

Jim picked Alexis up in one swoop as he carried her to the bedroom, responding: "You heard right, lady."

The couple ended up in an exhausted heap of sweat and some carnage after about twenty minutes.

"Still the only. Still the best," Jim teased.

"Wow," Alexis responded in earnest. "Wow!"

They fell asleep in each other's arms.

'Again, *the* team,' Alexis thought.

Chapter 42

Maracaibo, Venezuela
July 1944

Jim immediately regretted showing the top-secret notice to Alexis.

It was clear that she had finished reading. There were tears in her eyes; her face, at first white as a sheet, then turned an angry red.

Silently, Alexis laid the notice on the table — face up. She adjusted the corners so that the notice fit perfectly on the bottom right corner of the square table top.

She looked at Jim, walked quickly to the bathroom, closed the door, and threw up.

JAS — Your Eyes Only — Operation T-4 reactivation confirmed. Activity recently resumed. Death by injection of fatal dosage, or more often by starvation.

Jim had told Alexis about Hitler's Operation T-4. The 'T' was an abbreviation for the Berlin address, Tiergartenstrasse 4, from where the program was administered. The town of Hadamar, Germany, was the center of the beginning of German atrocities. Hadamar, in Hesse, close to Wiesbaden and about 50 miles northwest of Frankfurt, was the location of a former mental illness asylum, which evolved into a military hospital and in 1940 was transformed into an installation used for so-called euthanasia, pursuant to a direct written order signed by Hitler himself in October 1939.

T-4 had led to the extermination — murder— of roughly two-hundred-fifty thousand of the most vulnerable members of the German and Austrian populations, most of them non-Jews put to death with carbon monoxide gas, lethal injection, or starvation. About ten thousand of these were children. The Nazi dictatorship deemed all these human beings "lives unworthy to live," because they were considered a racial and financial burden on the German nation.

The so-called 'operations' started in the site at Hadamar, sitting atop of a hill in town, in mid-January 1941. A staff of one hundred physicians, nurses and assistants undertook the daily tasks of deception, killing, and cremation of patients transported to the facility by bus from around Hesse and the Prussian province of Hanover, as well as the southern German states of Baden-Württemberg and Bavaria. Through trickery and the selective use of force and sedatives, victims entered the facility, were told to undress, and place all their belongings in boxes to be recovered after the cleaning process. They were then funneled into the basement 'shower room', which was in fact just a gas chamber. They were then asphyxiated. The T-4 staff ensured that the bodies were immediately cremated, after which completely fabricated causes of death and the victim's ashes were then dispatched to their heartbroken family members.

The murder process was halted by Hitler on August 24, 1941, after the German public learned about the disappearance of men, women, and children with physical and mental disabilities. The gas chamber at Hadamar was quickly and quietly dismantled, after some ten thousand human beings had been murdered at the facility.

In the summer of 1942, the top-secret killings at Hadamar resumed, and this time — in coordination with Himmler — a new genocidal project, the extermination of European Jews. The killings continued until March 21, 1945, when the United States 2nd Infantry discovered and ended the killing machine of Hadamar. Only three Hadamar staff members were convicted of the atrocities and sentenced to death by the United States' military authorities. These devils were executed by hanging in March 1946.

However, all the above, up to this day of Jim's return, is not what warranted even more then throwing-up.

Just two months earlier, Jim was told by American officials that Jonathan's little sister (who was mentally deficient, and thus 'undesirable' in Nazi terms) had been forcibly taken from her family and delivered to Hadamar for 'better care and monitoring'. Carefully and professionally, Jim had immediately shared this information with Jonathan, but Jonathan already knew. He found out on the day Chloe was taken away. He had convinced himself that Chloe was in better hands with 'professionals', and that there would be others like her with whom she could socialize.

The final sentence of the short top-secret notice to Jim stated the following: "It is believed that one day prior to the date of this message, Major Jonathan Speer's younger sister Chloe was killed by lethal injection, cremated, and the family received the ashes with a note that Chloe had passed quietly in sleep. Family devastated."

Thirty minutes passed before Alexis would exit the bathroom.

Jim stood back up and opened his arms, and Alexis walked right in. He had tears in his eyes, and Alexis had more tears pouring down her cheeks. The two held each other tightly, swaying back and forth. They were sweating profusely from being in Maracaibo and very close to each other.

Alexis pushed gently away and fell on the couch. Jim sat himself on the floor right next to Alexis and massaged her back gently.

"You must leave and go tell Jonathan what you know. Maybe he does not know what you know. Maybe the message is incorrect, and Jonathan knows everything is ok. You must go now," Alexis whispered urgently.

"I cannot leave you when each of us is in a very sad state emotionally," Jim replied. "Let's just stay here a little longer and share how we feel or share nothing at all."

Alexis acquiesced.

The most either one of them knew about Chloe was that she was Jonathan's most beloved and loving little sister. He would talk about how he could not wait to return home to see her. It had already been two years since Jonathan was sent overseas. Chloe was six then — now, she would have been eight.

At home in Maracaibo, before home air-conditioners, you heard everything from the outside, and both Jim and Alexis heard a large car pull up to the house.

"Now what?" hissed Alexis.

Jim began walking to the front door as he heard a soft knock.

"It is Jonathan," Jim said softly. "We need to just listen. He knows, or else he would not be here right now."

Alexis hoped that was true, but only because if Jonathan had come to see her .... there would be an issue of significant proportion.

Jonathan looked as if he had run over to the house from downtown Maracaibo.

Jim opened his arms. For a moment, Jonathan just stood there in the entryway, as Jim reached around and closed the front door, primarily so the driver would not witness Jonathan wilt. Jonathan then strongly grabbed Jim and began to quietly cry. Alexis was now sitting up and just watching two grown men, both of whom she loved, grieving together.

Ordinarily, she would walk over and hug both of them. But she just felt awkward for the reasons she and the reader know.

"They killed Chloe, Jim," Jonathan said softly into Jim's right ear.

Jim said nothing, and just continued to hold his great friend Jonathan.

Jonathan sensed that Jim was aware of what had happened, and he said: "You knew?"

"As of two hours ago, Jonathan. For me to say I am sorry is just not enough. There is no way I can be as angry as you must feel toward those in Germany who identify as Nazi, but I am certainly as angry as I have ever been in my life. Will you please just come sit with Alexis and me and just talk and share? We are both here for you, and you know it."

Jonathan did not feel or act awkward sitting next to Alexis on the couch. Alexis took Jonathan's hand and held it to her eyes. Jim was just quietly exhausted while sitting across from the two on the couch. Jim's mind was racing with thoughts of how he could help. 'Did Jonathan want vengeance? How can I take advantage of this moment for the United States? Why am I even thinking that way? No, I need to think that way.'

"Jim, why does God allow this?" asked Jonathan timidly.

Whoa! Jim and Jonathan had never talked about their faiths before. Incidentally, neither had Alexis and Jonathan, but Jim would not know that — yet.

"I believe God is in control of everything, Jonathan. I believe He allows terrible things to happen, the purpose of which we cannot, at this moment in time, understand. So, I do not try. Chloe's death and my despair here is the most awful situation I have dealt with in my life, and yet I know Chloe did not die in vain. Her soul is too precious to God, otherwise Chloe could not have been and be the Chloe you knew and know. She could even be watching us now. It is up to us — absolutely nobody else — to do all we can muster to try to understand what Chloe would want us to do — or not do — at this point. This is what I believe, and I believe all of this very profoundly, Jonathan."

Alexis had never heard such a beautiful and sincere statement come from Jim's mouth. It was not so much the words, but the situation in which the words were spoken. As she held Jonathan's hand, she could feel him slow down, calm down, and exhale. She had never loved Jim more than during this moment, when he cared for another man she loved as much as she loved him.

Chapter 43

Maracaibo, Venezuela
August 1944

Alexis had to get away and think.

Jim and Jonathan had just left to go out into the countryside that Jonathan loved. The driver did not look into the eyes of either man, but he certainly knew his sole purpose in life at that moment was to just drive peacefully away from Maracaibo. He had been with the German Officer for two years. He knew him well.

Alexis quickly put on her sandals, walked outside, and headed up the local hill where one would go to hopefully enjoy some wind and peacefulness.

Alexis began talking to herself as she walked.

"So, here I am in Maracaibo, Venezuela. Over two-plus billion barrels of thick and dirty oil here. Not much else…I have concluded the following: I am worldly-wise and selectively worldly. Jim is worldly-wise and not worldly. Jonathan is worldly-wise, extremely worldly, and, surprisingly, a sensitive gentleman (at least with her, and now with her and Jim)."

"Who is the better person in the world at war?" Alexis continued to ask, talking to herself. "My Jim, my Jonathan, me? It is so complicated now. How did I get here? Did God allow all this to happen, as Jim would say, or are there darker powers (Satan) at work in Jonathan, Jim, and me as a group, or one or two of us, collectively or individually to destroy the good in the three of us? Clearly, my dear father Roy would have a calm and clear answer. He certainly dealt with these and even more complex issues as a conscientious objector and then a killer during WWI. Actually, he told me all about it, and the central theme of his talk to me strangely follows the same process I heard Jim state just now to Jonathan. Mother would just have thrown out any allowance for reasoning and would have said basically that all is black and white.

Looking at things as black and white certainly makes understanding life easier, but then why did God give us the ability to challenge and reason with what others see as clear opposites? God did not create us to be unwilling tools of anybody else. We must reason in order to understand God's love, His guidance, His greatness, His care (even for our smallest issues or roles in life) — just how He absolutely must have done for and with Chloe. Did Chloe understand she was God's child and God's instrument for a greater good? Probably not, but I do not know enough to be able to say she did not. So, she must have. Oh, to put myself in her place, watching the evil eyes of her killer locate the correct vein in which to place the needle laced with death. Just thinking like this right now is destroying me. It is too much to bear."

At that moment Alexis reached the top of the hill, felt the light wind surround her now weakened body, and she softly fell into the one clump of grass near her. She cried again.

She continued her emotional and mental journey into the unknown.

"I need to open-up to Jim about my role in all this — that is, how the OSS has me even watching him. Of course, I would have married him even without the direction of the OSS. We were already engaged when they approached me and told me I had a duty not to let him know that I too was searching for information about the Nazis' work in South America. But my duty is to Jim, not the OSS. Jim and I will talk about this tonight. However, I cannot tell Jim about Jonathan and me. Not now, and maybe not ever. Am I really in love with Jonathan and Jim? Awkward, but both meaningful to me, and necessary for my country. I did not plan to fall in love with Jonathan, and I knew I would never fall out of love with Jim. It just so happens I love each and both. That is all I need to deal with for now about this matter."

At this moment, Alexis felt a soft tapping on her left shoulder. She sat up and opened her eyes to see this little boy, maybe six years old, looking directly into Alexis' soul, and smiling from ear to ear. He was dusty and dirty like any little boy would be on a day like this, on a hill like this, in a country like this. The boy had a fresh banana in his right hand and offered the banana to Alexis. He was too young to know what was going on in Alexis' eyes, but he was not too young to care enough to offer an item of care, at just the right moment.

Alexis reached out and softly took the offering, placed it gently on the ground, and reached up with both hands to hold the little boy's head, tussle his hair and tweak his nose.

"Muchas gracias, estimado joven," said Alexis with sound respect in her voice.

The boy smiled, blew Alexis a kiss, ran further up the hill and disappeared.

"Was that an angel, my own angel, a little boy, or all three?" mused Alexis.

"All three," she quickly concluded. She noticed she was relaxed, more comfortable, and she had a small smile.

"Thank you, my God, for You and for Your letting me be me, while honoring You," she whispered to herself as she leisurely walked home downhill.

Jim returned very late that night. He was exhausted. Alexis had left four large fresh chocolate chip cookies on the kitchen table. There was always an accompanying note, but none more sincere and meaningful as this.

My dear husband Jim —

I am so proud of you and how you handled the entire episode today regarding Jonathan and his darling sister Chloe. If I am asleep when you get home, it was not easy. I missed you. I know that Jonathan is thankful for your deep and nurturing friendship.

So glad you are mine.

Lovingly,

Lexi [only Jim and Roy were allowed to use this nickname]

Jim rinsed off in the lukewarm water ending up as a cold shower. There were no water heaters in Maracaibo homes at the time. The water filled the roof water tank during the day. The hot sun warmed it. As you showered and got lathered up, the warm water slowly turned cool. The water is pumped up from the well near the house. Nevertheless, you were clean, and the bed was warm and damp anyway. Yuck.

Chapter 44

Maracaibo, Venezuela
August 1944

"Wake up Jim! Wake up! We need to go right away."

It was a man's voice. "Really?" Jim whimpered.

"Really, Jimbo. Now!"

It was Jonathan. Why?

"Where is Alexis?" Jim mumbled, in an aggravated way.

"She is throwing together a quick breakfast for us. This is urgent, and we need to move now. I will explain in the car. The driver is outside. He knows nothing about what is going on. Move!"

Jim knew he had heard all he needed to hear. He quickly got out of bed, visited the rest room, brushed his hair and teeth, got dressed in Saturday garb (even though it was Wednesday), and scurried to the Kitchen.

"Good morning, Lexi," Jim said as he hugged his wife.

Jonathan shuddered. 'Lexi! Why did I not think of that? Perfect for my Alex. And, I like Alex better anyway. Lexi is too feminine for a woman such as Alexis,' Jonathan reasoned.

Both men hammered down three eggs over easy (Jonathan hated over easy, and Alex knew that), two pieces of toast, and a small bowl of mango slices. Some water. A short statement of thanks to Lexi/Alex/Alexis or no name at all. Gone.

Chapter 45

Maracaibo, Venezuela
August 1944

"Yeow! Jonathan. It is 6 a.m.!" Jim exclaimed.
"Jim, I forget. Do you know French?"
"No."
"Mandarine?"
"No."
"Latin?"
"Yes."
"Never mind, I was terrible at Latin. Whispers in English, then. No more talking until we get on the plane," Jonathan concluded.

"We are headed to the far end of the Maracaibo airport. There is an unmarked British aircraft waiting for us. Motors running. We are headed to the mouth of the Orinoco River in eastern Venezuela. No stops. By the way, no head on this plane either. There is a hose."

Jim knew all the British-made planes and had flown in most of them. He thought each was terrifically made. But not one was comfortable, and he now was sure that Jonathan, he, and the unfortunate pilot would be crammed into a British Mosquito.

As the driver pulled into the airport and drove quickly to the mostly unused western portion of the airport, Jim saw the form of the famed British Mosquito — "Ugh! Not pressurized and no head."

The plane is made for two, plus bombs. Jim, being just a little smaller than Jonathan, would end up lying flat in the bomb bay for the entire trip, likely two-hours.

"How long is the trip?" asked Jonathan of the sole pilot.

"Just shy of three and a half hours, sir," responded the pilot.

"Aye!" exclaimed Jim as he laid down with his head near the pilot's seat.

"I thought this plane was fast," Jim yelled at the pilot.

"It is. That's why it will only take the time I told you." The pilot yelled back.

"Is there a relief hose here in the bomb bay?" cried Jim.

"Nope," the pilot and Jonathan replied in unison.

Jonathan leaned down and spoke loudly to Jim. The plane had just taken off and was climbing. The twin motors did not strain at all.

"Once we reach altitude, around seven thousand, we can talk."

Jim just rolled away in disgust.

The Mosquito was unique among WWII fighters because it was made primarily of wood, mostly balsa wood, not metal. Like a U-boat covered with some type of rubber, it was hard to detect, only in this case on radar.

The Royal Air Forces' (RAF) fast bomber first flew in November of 1940. In order to keep detectability and weight down, the speedy plane was constructed primarily of spruce, birch plywood, and balsa wood. This building method had the added bonus of preserving war-critical duralumin and steel for other military aircraft projects. The Mosquito was powered by a pair of Rolls-Royce Merlin V-12 engines, similar to those seen in the RAF's Spitfire and Hurricane.

The Mosquito became one of the fastest (maximum speed of 378 MPH), far-flying (1,855 miles), highest ceiling (33,000 feet, with a rate of climb of 1,740 ft/min), and most versatile aircraft of WWII. Without changing design, these planes served as bombers, fighters, fighter-bombers, night fighters, and reconnaissance planes.

"Still not fast enough," was Jim's sole commentary that morning. He fell back asleep and was out the entire trip.

For Jonathan the plane was too loud. He had forgotten the Mosquito had the two V12 engines, and he wished he had brought his ear plugs.

Chapter 46

Orinoco River Basin, Venezuela
August 1944

It was the middle of dry season, and the pilot was sure they could find a hard enough dry part of the river up near the Atlantic mouth. He was right, and he did, quickly turning off the engines to conserve fuel.

"Ok, blokes. We are here. Did you enjoy the flight?" Both Jim and Jonathan jumped out and headed to the large dry bush near what was probably the high tide west bank.

"Thank you, Tiger (that was the pilot's given name)," Jonathan answered. "Did you receive any directions from my driver on what to bring?"

"Yes," replied Tiger. "I will get the stuff right now."

Tiger opened the lower compartment door of the plane and pulled out what looked like all that Jonathan had requested.

"A shovel, two American M1911s, one American M1 Garand, two Sykes knives (a favorite Allied double edge fighting knife), six American grenades, and two Thompson submachine guns." Tiger announced proudly. "Oh, and a whole bunch of ammo for all the guns. I cleaned these all myself. When not flying, of course."

"Oh, and the flare gun. Two red and two blue flares. Actually, you ordered two each, I have three each — just in case."

"Good pilot and a thinker as well. Thank you. I hope the clothes kind of fit," Jim quipped as he got dressed. The clothes were British desert outfits — just perfect.

"Excellent job, Tiger," Jim said as he was putting on the clothes. "Well done, Jonathan, as well. We are well equipped, especially the knife." Jim loved knives and was an excellent high-grade knife fighter. In addition to military training, Jim learned street tactics in Pontiac, Michigan, at Rufus' Bar. The OSS adopted what tactics Jim showed them from Pontiac. However, Jim did not at all enjoy looking into a man's eyes or hold him as he killed him. "It is awful to kill by hand," Jim would tell Alex as he taught her. "The body becomes heavier and more awkward as the soul leaves, Lexi. Use the pistol, if at all possible," Jim would add.

"Ok, I better get going," Tiger said as he looked at his watch.

Jonathan nodded as Tiger said this.

"What?" said a very surprised and annoyed Jim.

"I am sorry we could not talk on the plane, Jim," Jonathan said quickly. "You slept anyway. Tiger has enough petrol to circle at a low speed for around three hours. My watch says straight-up noon. Tiger, unless we flare you, be back here right at 3:00 p.m."

"Now get out of here before they get here," commanded Jonathan.

"What?" Jim once again asked, getting more upset that he did not know everything, nor anything, really.

Tiger cranked each engine over and was gone.

"Ok, Jim, here is why I had to grab you. Without any discussion right now, please. I am no longer a Nazi, and I will renounce my German citizenship as soon as possible — that is if we are alive after this."

Jim hid his delight at this news for now.

Jonathan continued, somewhat disappointed that Jim had not jumped up and down with pleasure at the news. It was Jim who has been pushing this onto Jonathan for at least the last two years. "Was Jim now not interested?"

Figure 12: A crocodile lying on the edge of the Orinoco river in the jungle.

"If I were not upset with you right now about being here, I would give you a big hug. That is good news, Jonathan. You could, however, have told me this without bringing me here," teased Jonathan. "Why are we here?"

"Jim, one of Germany's newest U-boats, U-476 to be precise, is just off the coast. No, they cannot see us individually. They are still submerged. They are waiting at periscope level for my signal.

Jim was a 'ready-aim-fire' kind of man. Jonathan was more 'ready-fire-aim'. Each method generally worked well for each man. This was now, however, a time to think. And that is what Jim was doing.

"Jonathan, the Orinoco mouth is over seven miles wide and in parts over two-hundred feet deep, certainly deep enough for a U-boat to drive right up the river at periscope depth. I pray he did not do that and is watching us now. Let's get into the brush right away." Jim was loading up as he talked, and Jonathan followed suit. "I know this area well," Jim added.

The Orinoco River is the second longest and widest river in South America. It flows out of Brazil, and through Colombia and Venezuela until it empties into the Atlantic Ocean near Trinidad. It contains over one thousand species of animals, including the world's longest anacondas, its own very dangerous and carnivorous Orinoco crocs, sharks at its mouth (primarily dangerous hammerheads), and, for your pleasure, piranha (which eat just about everything very quickly, especially flesh from mammals).

Jim continued. "Why are they here and when did you set all this up?"

"I received the call the night before we heard about my sister. They have a troublemaker on board who I have been asked to take out immediately. He is the son of some German mucketymuck. They asked me to find a reason to shoot him, and I just might."

"Did they say anything about needing fuel? They have about one-hundred barrels of diesel around that bend over there." Jonathan shook his head.

"Jonathan, this does not look right. I have to trust you, as I always do. Is there any chance you are being used to get me here? Also, they are going to have to use a dingy to get him ashore. It is muddy, but there are large anacondas, the famous, fast, and very dangerous and carnivorous Orinoco crocodiles that weigh up to eight-hundred-and-fifty pounds, can get up to eighteen feet long and have been around for over two-hundred million years, plus sharks in that water. Big crocs, little hammerheads. Both are deadly."

"I am not hurt, Jim. I was waiting for you to ask something like you just did. No, I am done as a Nazi — I swear on Chloe's grave! That should do it!"

"It does," answered Jim gravely.

The two men were in the bushes laying out their weapons. Jonathan reached for the flare gun.

Jim grabbed Jonathan's arm and took both of them to the ground. "Here it comes!"

Jim figured things were ok for the moment. 'If the U-boat Captain thought it was a trap, he would not be piloting slowly toward the mouth and up the river a little. But there was something wrong,' thought Jim.

"You said this boat is new? It sure looks just like the others. But … it is quiet. Very quiet. And there is exhaust, with the engines running! It is a shiny grey — not black as all your — their — other U-boats."

"There is the captain, plus three others just now getting on the bridge. The three are using their glasses, and looking North, West, and East. They must be confident they are alone — only the captain is looking down the river. Jonathan, take the pistol and your knife, that is all. Act casual, take the hate out of your eyes, and start heading their way. Hurry!"

Jim was hurriedly stripping down to his birthday suit. "I am going to have to get in the water."

"But Jim … why? You said there were …." Jonathan said with anxiousness and concern.

"I know. Go!"

Jim grabbed his knife, and quickly and quietly headed the opposite direction from Jonathan, sliding quietly into the water. The U-boat was about seventy-five yards away, and the current was thankfully slow. 'The tide is slowly coming in,' thought Jim. The water was coming in from the Atlantic, and gently carried Jim toward the U-boat. The sailors on the bridge only just saw Jonathan. All four men on the bridge looked excitedly at him, as if they had been lost and Jonathan had found them.

They yelled at each other in German. Jim never told Jonathan that Jim knew fluent German. As a spy, leverage is necessary, and people should know as little about you as possible. And, based on what was being said, the captain just was happy with himself for finding the correct river ('Kind of hard to miss,' Jim thought, 'Its mouth is over thirty-four miles wide, and the Orinoco is the second largest River in South America.'), glad to see Jonathan, and wanted to get right back out to sea. The three sailors started watching for planes, but there were none. The front top hatch opened, and a very small dingy was placed outside. Out came a young sailor. The hatch closed, the sailor climbed immediately into the dingy and started rowing toward shore and Jonathan.

Suddenly, the U-boat reversed, and the bridge was cleared. The back top hatch opened and a sailor with a rifle climbed out and looked Jim right in the eyes. He raised the rifle and shot as Jim slipped under the water. The sailor leaned over to see if there was any blood. The sub lurched; the sailor fell into the water with the rifle. Somebody reached out and slammed the hatch closed right as water was rising over the top. Jim surfaced, and immediately afterward, his enemy surfaced five feet away.

Jim was already back underwater. Suddenly, the enemy was pulled under. Jim slit the sailor's throat and then jammed the dagger into his temple, all in one smooth move. The best knife fight lasts no longer than forty-five seconds. This one lasted five. Lots of blood. Jim quickly pushed off, and started swimming as fast as he could to shore — and away from the blood. He had just seen a croc, at least ten feet long, surface and head toward the blood. Suddenly there was more surface movement over near the bloody body. Jim looked back towards the shore. Ten feet to go and he could feel his feet touching the river floor. Then he was up running toward Jonathan. His heel hurt like crazy. You do not rest on the shore when crocs are looking for something unique to eat. The Orinoco croc can run faster than a man for a short distance — the powerful tail pushes the croc forward and then the feet just move even faster.

Jonathan had pulled the young German sailor out of the dinghy, shot holes into the small boat and pushed it back into the river. Then he hurriedly ran toward Jim and away from the river. He left the sailor on his own. 'Who cares?' thought Jonathan. He was in no mood to kill the sailor now. Let the crocs or whatever do it.

It did not matter; the sailor was scared enough, and he was just now passing Jonathan and entered the jungle. Jim and Jonathan met where their weapons were. They grabbed everything, and Jonathan just grabbed the sailor by his shirt, and then all three ran deeper into the jungle.

They saw a small clearing and stopped. All this must have taken no more than six minutes.

"Jim, there is a baby hammerhead hanging on to your left heel." Jonathan said calmly.

Jim worked the shark off and threw it into the jungle in disgust.

"You are fortunate it did not bite off your...."

Jim held up his hand, and between breaths, he began to spread his arms wide, and stated "it is too ..."

"Small" finished Jonathan with a concerned snarl.

"That is what I was going to say," came out of the sailor's mouth.

Jonathan looked at the sailor, "You speak ..."

"Unwisely," finished Jim.

Jonathan stretched above the heavy leaves and saw that the U-boat was just out of the river and heading farther out. It had quit descending, but water was just below the top of the conning tower, and the U-boat continued to head out ... but it was also watching.

"Jonathan. Signal the plane with the red flare. Hurry. That means to just head back our way and not land — correct?"

"Yes sir," Jonathan quipped back.

"Good. When the U-boat sees the plane, it will head straight out to deeper water! I hope!"

Jim continued pulling on his pants and lacing his boots. No shirt.

Up went the flare.

All was quiet. The sailor was truly scared. Jonathan and Jim were sweating all over, and very nervous. What if the U-boat had planned on meeting somebody while it was here? Are there soldiers around here? Had a landing party formed?

Jonathan and Jim stood back-to-back, machine guns loaded, unlocked, and hanging from their sides. Jim also shouldered his M1 Garand. Jonathan put a pistol in his belt, as did Jim. Jim pushed 'sailor boy' down into the grass and signaled the young man to stay or die. It was in Jim's eyes. Jonathan used parts of a torn shirt to tie the sailor's hands behind his back.

All three were breathing hard.

Nobody was out there, and the U-boat was at least underwater, right below its periscope depth. No landing party — yet. Somebody was still monitoring the river mouth.

And then, here came Tiger. Low and loud. Certainly, he could not see the U-boat or its periscope. The water was so damn muddy. But, if he made noise, he would scare somebody, and that could only help the good guys at the moment.

Surprisingly, the periscope was steady.

"Is Tiger's plane armed?" questioned Jonathan.

Jonathan shook his head.

Jim was thinking hard. He wanted to tear off Jonathan's head! 'Not armed???' They needed to get back on that plane before the U-boat captain had time to think. All Jim and Jonathan needed was a landing party coming after them, or the U-boat surfacing and shooting its forward deck machine gun at the men and the plane!'

"Send up the blue flare, pointing down river. Now!"

Up went the blue flare. In no time, Tiger did another flyover at about one-hundred feet, circled and headed down for the landing.

"When he touches down, we run toward him as fast as we can. Jonathan, you and I both need to catch Tiger's eyes and signal for him to point the plane down river, away from the U-boat. Once the Captain sees us running, he is going to try to surface enough to use his forward thirty-millimeter gun — because he will know a plane is coming for us, not him."

Tiger's plane hit the hard riverbank, and off went the three wet men. The plane slowed, turning down-river. The bomb bay opened, the two props were trimmed, and the motors were idling fast … clearly it would be more expedient for the men to climb up the bomb bay. And up all three went. Jim gave Tiger the thumbs up as the plane began to move and the bay doors began to close.

Off the plane went down the riverbank. It was airborne and well down the river in thirty seconds. It climbed quickly into the sun, and it was gone.

"Who is the 'newbie'?" chirped Tiger. Jonathan, Jim, and the newbie were lying down all over each other and looking up. Exhausted and alive … and, Jim had just learned something very important. 'That's it! The U-boat was covered with a rubber coating! That's why it was so quiet and a shiny grey color rather than black.' Jim thought to himself.

Jonathan untied the newbie's hands.

There were what seemed like hundreds of small urchins and leaches on and in Jim's pants. Without thought, he took off all his clothing, and threw it toward the back of the plane. He placed a snake-like creature next to Jonathan's leg. He sat there naked, nobody looked, and nobody cared. Fortunately, they had each put their dry clothes in the plane after the earlier changeover to kakis.

Chapter 47

Maracaibo, Venezuela
August 1944

"I am getting very tired of the long days such as this where the men, yes, my men, trudge off early toward and into danger," Alexis said out loud to herself. "I would rather be with them right now. I am pretty good at this stuff too — as I have already proven to each of them."

By now, Alexis was angry and getting more so every minute.

She took out some pieces of paper, grabbed a pen, and tried to think of happier times only last week. She was remembering when only a few weeks ago, she had spent most of the day in bed with Jonathan.

But the most meaningful event of the day happened that night. She had been thinking about a poem she proposed to give to Jonathan last week. The night she took him dancing in the fountain in the middle of the plaza Jonathan and she loved.

And she 'wrestled' in bed with Jonathan, while her husband Jim was off truly wrestling with the Nazi Germans in another way — and each was at that time serving their country.

Were they, therefore, serving God as well?

It is clear that the resounding answer was 'yes' — we as a nation were in a global battle against evil empires (Nazi Germany and Imperial Japan). Battles are messy and complex. That is the nature of these things.

Chapter 48

Maracaibo, Venezuela
August 1944

Jim got back home at 4:00 a.m., very tired. He quickly showered and climbed into bed naked. Wow. Climbing into bed next to absolutely beautiful and sexy Alexis is such an enormous treat that God gave to Jim. Jim knew that Jonathan was at around the same time climbing into bed, probably with a new pretty woman who most likely was mad at him for not being there earlier that night. She was probably not aware of what Jonathan likely really needed right now.

Jim's wife knew exactly what to do, and how to do it. She acted asleep until Jim got comfortable. She rolled over toward him and climbed onto his strong, tan, and tense body. Their eyes were locked as Alex lightly massaged between Jim's legs. She had just earlier prepared her nails to do what Jim loves being done to him.

"Hi mister. Are you comfortable?" Alexis was slowly taking off her skimpy light blue silk nightgown and continued with her eyes on Jim's eyes the entire time."

"What is your name?" Jim asked as he reached up to lightly massage the lady's tender but strong shoulders. "You certainly look like and act like the most beautiful and giving wife in the world."

"Oh, you have heard of me?"

"Lady, I have studied your body for over six years. I hope that someday, before I wake up from this dream, you tell me your name!

By now, Jim was as hard as he had ever been. The lady continued to massage him, and Jim would lightly moan to show his appreciation."

"My name is Mrs. Barclay, which is exactly how they told me to be with you right now." Alexis dove into Jim. They began to wrestle teasingly and passionately. Jim was touching everything in just the right way and at just the right time. He focused entirely on Alexis, which excited him even more.

"Stop!" Alex firmly commanded. She used her hands to adjust Jim onto his back, with his arms to his side. "Do not move!"

Jim obeyed.

Slowly and passionately, Alexis used every part of her body to work for Jim's pleasure, as she whispered into Jim's ears: "I was made for your pleasure. Relax and enjoy."

Jim did and he did.

Suddenly, Jim opened his eyes, reached out and took Alexis's face with both hands. "Who taught you all this!" Jim asked firmly.

Alexis stopped completely and placed her right hand tenderly on Jim's mouth and whispered: "Shhhh."

She sat there on Jim's groin for about a minute. Then she slowly leaned down to Jim's left ear. She blew into his ear, and gently placed her tongue inside.

"My husband did."

That was all Jim needed, and he shuddered.

Chapter 49

Maracaibo, Venezuela
September 1944

Jonathan had to drop the young sailor off at the brig behind the American Embassy. He had just gotten home, stumbled into the shower and stood under the cool water for a minute or two, lathered up, rinsed off, and got out of there. A quick dry-off and into his soft white linen. He laid on his back and stared at the ceiling.

"A lot going on, Jonathan. Stay steady and smart."

He was alone in his bed. She apparently came on time but did not stick around. Jonathan was alone in his bed, again.

With that thought he fell asleep.

The sailor rolled over on the metal cot in his hot damp cell. He thought of a woman as well — what will he tell his mother.

Chapter 50

Maracaibo, Venezuela
September 1944

Jim ignored the your-eyes-only weekend satchel that is delivered at 8:30 p.m. every Friday by a U.S. Embassy messenger. The messenger changes his disguise every day. He was the milkman last night. Nevertheless, Alex had laid the satchel next to Jim on the bed. So, he opened it out of guilt. Not much in there but a sealed note from the Marine security force. Jim opened the envelope and read the note:

For-your-eyes-only — December 17, 1943
Jim — I hope you are doing well. I cannot believe you went on a mission with Jonathan and Tiger, and then bring a gift for me to watch (yes, he is now with us). I do not mean to be comical at this time. You asked me to watch for anything with information about your family and close friends related to war casualties. You already know that Timothy Clausen and Paul Broach were killed in combat last month. The most recent casualty is one Bobby Wymore, again a classmate of yours at Pontiac MI. He was killed in battle on Bougainville, S.I. on December 15, 1943. The Higgins boat he was piloting in the first wave of the landing on Bougainville was hit by shell fire. All thirty-six Marines were instantly killed. He died fighting for his country.
Major General Collison

Jim buried his head in his pillow. He spent time thinking about the great times he and Bobby had. They both loved the sciences, and they messed around in the chemistry lab all the time. He had signed up to fight because he always wanted to be a Marine. He was a superior person. After he graduated from Princeton, Bobby fell in love with a woman named Daisy Messmore, who was quite older than he, but they were deeply in love.

Bobby and Daisy got married just before Bobby was shipped out to the South Pacific. He kept telling Daisy that he would be alright because he was responsible for taking his fellow Marines to the battle, and then he just turned around for more Marines still on the ship. Daisy had told Alex that was her worry — Bobby was still a Marine no matter what his job was. If he felt the battle needed him, he would be there with his buddies.

Jim decided not to tell Alexis at this time about Bobby's death. There was enough sadness around right now. Chloe's death really depressed all of them.

Instead, Jim went into the little kitchen, found paper and pen, and he began to write. He would often write poetry as a way to respond to stress and depression or exceeding joy. This was certainly not a time of happiness. Jim scribbled the poem below. He made some assumptions in an attempt to express the impact of Bobby's death on his young wife and others.

Daisy and Bobby
Jim Barclay — September 1944

Bullets and mortars,
And so, so much noise,
Pieces of metal fly by,
And into the bodies of our brave boys.

These hellish little islands,
Held by those of the Rising Sun,

They will hold them no longer,
They are now on the run.

All around me,
My friends are dying or dead,
I am 30 years young,
Watching so much death by lead.

It is December 15, 1943,
I see "Sammy", "Turk"
"Jimmy" and "Tree",
"Preacher" and "Boo"
They are now dead.
Suddenly, I am dead too.

I am above the battle,
I am looking down,
I had felt nothing,
Like they say when you drown.

I see my body,
Parts of it all around,
And the boat I was driving,
Has just run aground.

My first thought is Daisy,
Then Mother and Dad,
They will feel pain,
They will be sad.

This will hurt all three,
As they think about me.

This just happened,
I just died,
They said there was glory in battle,
But they had lied.

I hear her voice,
And my Daisy approaches,
We were …,
Each other's choices.

Why is she near me,
How is this done,
Here there is no time,
No clock to run.

As she always did,
She whispers in my ear,
"I am now with you,
I am now here."

"When we were married,
You had told me of this,
But it made no sense then,
I was lost in our kiss."

"Later, it was 2020,
I was 100 years old,
When I headed your way,
I had just fallen down,
I had begun to sway."

"As I laid where I fell,
And then as I died,
I knew this would happen,
While the relatives cried."

"Yes, I remarried,
But I was always yours."

"He understood,
He knew about this,
I was able to love him,
But he and I never had our kiss."

"Now you and I are one,
And this is now done,
We can walk together forever,
Into the sun."

I reach for her hand,
As she reaches for mine,
Together again at last,
In the place of no time."

Chapter 51

The Kehlsteinhaus (a.k.a. The Eagle's Nest), on Obersalzberg Mountain, Germany
October 1944

Hitler was not feeling well.

It was a hazy winter morning and the party of the evening before was wonderful. The guests were each excited to spend time with the Führer. One of the guests was Schneider.

Yes, he was attractive, smart, well versed in the affairs of this war, and eager to serve the Third Reich and its leader – but Hitler and Himmler had their quiet doubts about whether Schneider could get the oil commitment from the Venezuelans, as well the natural rubber for the submarines in time to turn the tide of the war for Germany.

Some background -- Around early 1944, the English developed sonar (code names "High Tea"). Critical to the success of the Allies against the stealthy U-boats was the sonar technology where any ship could monitor the bastion killer beneath the surface of the sea by bouncing a sound off of hidden killer's steel infrastructure – the "ping-like" sound flowing back to the sonar operator's ears.

Without the German U-boats sinking Allied sources of supplies, things started going very badly for the Third Reich. In early 1945, the Germans responded with a powerful solution, basically, a way to reduce and even eliminate the ping related to sonar. The solution was to wrap U-Boats with natural rubber (Germany at one time early in the war was a large producer of synthetic rubber, but the synthetic rubber did not absorb the ping well, it would not adhesive reliably onto the U-boats, and, most of the synthetic plants were nearing destruction by highly effective Allied bombers).

Hitler enjoyed managing his personal war against the world. But things had not gone well with the critical U-Boat branch of his Navy. The sinking of ships was always dramatic, and Hitler insisted that pictures of these events be shared with him. However, as soon as the English invented sonar as a means to find and destroy the secretive U-Boats, all the Allies utilized this scientific marvel to find and kill Hitler's most destructive force and, particularly, all the ships bringing supplies for the English and other Allies – particularly that nuisance "save the world" country called the United States of America.

Venezuela had everything Germany needed. Venezuela declared itself neutral early in the war, but, behind the scenes, Venezuela would not make a move without getting proper authorization from the American government.

So, the oil linkage and the sending of natural rubber to Germany was necessarily done on the sly. The last sly shipment intended for Portugal for the benefit of the Axis powers was already in operation in October 1944.

Hitler had asked his neighbor and top military leader and advisor, Heinrich Himmler, to join him that morning on the sun porch at the Eagle's Nest. Staff and guests were always advised not to bother Hitler when he was meeting with his senior advisors on this sun porch. It was solidly private, and afforded an expansive view of the valley two thousand feet below and the mountains up to two hundred miles distant.

When Himmler arrived on the sun porch, Hitler appeared deep in thought – the nature of which required silence from his guest until Hitler spoke.

"What did you think of Schneider last evening" asked the Fuhrer to his top military commander Himmler.

"Well, I was jealous of all of the attention Schneider received from all the attractive and unattractive women. But, he is no longer one of our suspects for the leaked secrets regarding our intentions in South America, primarily Venezuela," was Heinrich Himmler's response.

"But what of the oil and natural rubber?" questioned Hitler.

"Heinrich, if you are unhappy with Schneider, get somebody else! We have no time for games. Our empire will fail if we are unable to access South American oil, food, natural resources, manpower, metal riches … and natural rubber" hissed Hitler.

"I understand, and we are just about to receive a significant amount of fresh natural rubber. The rubber is set on barges which are currently making their way down the Orinoco River, and then onto an ocean-going barge to Portugal. Finally, the rubber will be sufficient enough to cover thirty-five of our newest U-boats, will be driven -- mostly at night to avoid the likeliness of fierce air attacks along the way – our U-Boat facilities to France, where our rubber teams are waiting with 30 submarines for rubber covering" said Himmler.

"What is taking so long?" Hitler asked impatiently.

"Mein Fuhrer, navigating through the smaller river tributaries of the fierce Orinoco River, is extremely difficult and dangerous, and Schneider has developed deep ties with the indigenous tibes who are the only ones who know how to navigate through the River to the Orinoco's mouth. There the rubber will be transferred to a Portuguese cargo boat and brought to us. He has spent significant time developing the relationships — lots of time and money" stated Himmler.

"What about the spy among us?" Hitler said with a strong hateful tone.

"We originally thought that the spy was Schneider. It is not him – it is his cousin Jonathan Speer. Part of this mission is to question, torture and eliminate Speer. Remember? Speer is the one we originally assigned to the American OSS spies – Jim and Alexis Braclay?" Himler asked.

"I understand Jim Barclay is an urgent, violent and relentless opponent of ours. I like him," Hitler stated.

"And of course, the lovely Alexis Barclay – a.k.a. the missionary's wife. Some wife! We got Jonathan to spy on Alexis and Jim, and the Americans got Alexis to spy on Jonathan. I assume Alexis and Jim will be terminated as well after we get what we need?" Hitler asked.

There was a quiet pause, and then Himmler proceeded.

"I thought you wanted Jim and Jonathan terminated, but Alexis brought back alive to you for your intellectual and sexual pleasure. It has all been arranged." Himmler stated with foul pride only felt by a human of the lowest level of dignity and ethics.

"I have never met a woman as Alexis has been described to me by Schneider and others. She is elegant, sophisticated, smart, beautiful and sexy, intellectual, a swift killer and a liar. I knew Jonathan was in over his head. What a shame. But yes, you are correct, all three need to be executed – eventually." Hitler smiled.

Hitler liked both Schneider and Speer. At large parties, a group would often play the game of being the first to locate these two finest of specimens of the Arian race. Speer was handsome and Schneider was "devilishly" cute. They had identical body build, and people would swear that from the back, you could not distinguish which one was who.

There was a long silence. Hitler moved to the terrace and looked out over the magnificent Ural mountains.

"Us getting the natural oil commitment from the Venezuelan's and the natural rubber from the Orinoco jungles to the seaports in Portugal, are most likely the most significant events that need to take place before the end of December of this year (1944) in order for us to succeed in this war," said Hitler in a prophetic sort of way.

"If we had initially been able to capture the Venezuelan oil fields and the Aruban and Curacao refineries, we would be in a significantly better place than we are now. We will make this work, Mein Fuhrer," said Himmler.

"How is our gold?" Hitler asked.

"Safely submerged, Mein Hitler!" Himmler lied in response. He was very concerned that to date, two U-Boats stocked full of stolen riches were unaccounted for.

Hitler stood in silence for over three minutes, and then raised his arm as if to shoe Himmler off the porch.

Himmler, on the other hand, raised his right arm in the traditional salute to Hitler, clicked his heals, and he was gone.

"Before executing either Alexis or Jim Barclay or Jonathan Speer, we must get the location of the two lost U-Boats!" Himmler said to himself. He dreaded the day Hitler would be told that the U-Boats are not accounted for.

Chapter 52

Maracaibo, Venezuela
September 1944

At 6:00 a.m. sharp the next morning, there was a knock at the front door. Jim pulled his arms out from around Lexi, got up and put on his light summer robe. He had an idea who this was at the door.

"Good morning, Jonathan." In the Nazi stumbled.

"Coffee?"

"Not yet, sorry."

"OK, I will make some for you. Jim, go get some clothes on. Just weekend clothes."

Jonathan headed right to the kitchen as if he had been there before. He knew where the beans and the grinder were, the coffee dripper, and the sugar.

At about the same moment, Jim noticed Jonathan's acquaintance with the Barclay kitchen, and Jonathan noticed that Jim noticed. Neither said a word, as Jim headed to the bedroom for clothes and to wash his face.

Alexis was awake. Jim kissed her on the forehead.

"Good morning, Angel. Jonathan is here. I do not know exactly why, but we truly need to chat about some matters we became aware of yesterday."

Figure 13: Alexis, Jim, and Jonathan eye each other suspiciously across the dining room table in the Barclay residence.

"OK," Alexis mumbled as she dropped her head back down on the damp pillow — but, of course, everything was damp in their house, and everybody else's. Maracaibo!

It never took Jim any time to wake up and get moving at any time of the twenty-four-hour day.

"More news about Chloe?" Jim asked as he pulled out the chair and sat down at the table.

"No. It is about yesterday. We pulled off a small miracle .... no, a huge one! One minutes' difference in any direction of our time on the shore could have destroyed the two of us. Read the telex I received a half hour ago.

U-boat 481 surfaced to head to the fuel dump. Noticed a naked man on shore. Looked British or American. We headed right toward this man we thought worked for Major Speer. In one minute or less, the naked man dove into the water at the same moment the men in the front torpedo room pushed the Wolfgang child out the front hatch and onto the dingy. While surfaced, one sailor in back saw the naked man in the water and started shooting. We think he missed, and the naked man got eaten anyway — only a crazy man or a person who does not know the area would dive into that water. We dove as quickly as possible and got out of there. There was what appeared to be a British Mosquito passing over. It dove at us but did not shoot. We will stay below for forty-eight hours and then go get fuel.

Jim knew the answer, but exclaimed: "Where is there fuel out there? What are they talking about?"

Jonathan looked into Jim's eyes as he rolled his. "Jim. Really?"

Jim leaned back in the chair and looked at the ceiling. There were two tarantulas up there. Charlie the scorpion, a regular, had not yet arrived.

"What does this all mean for each of us now? We need to think."

"Should I make some pancakes gentlemen?"

She had not fixed herself up but looked beautiful to both men anyway.

"Please," Jim stated. "I will make better coffee."

"Query — who is this young man Wolfgang? Do you think they saw you even though they said they did not? Was a trap being set to catch me and .... never mind ... did they load up with fuel? Was there a Nazi shore party to catch or kill whoever? Is this telex a trap…but a trap to get who?

"And who was the naked American in the water, married I suppose, leaving a young wife in this hot foreign country," Alex chirped in a rather mean way.

She looked straight into Jim's eyes: "There are huge crocs and a billion hammerheads where this man swam!"

"He caught one … or should I say one caught him," added Jonathan with a smile.

Suddenly, the room went quiet. During the awkward silence, each person in the room realized that the other two were also in the room, and some secrets were suddenly out. What just happened?

"We could agree to shoot each other …" Jim said with a strange smile.

"Not in my kitchen!" Lexi scolded.

Jonathan did not know what to do. Neither did Jim. Neither did Alexis. There was an awkward silence.

So, nothing was done, perhaps because enough had been done.

Alexis tried to immediately change the topic.

"Ok. Time to play out-do each other's clever and credible battle sayings. I will start. 'If the enemy is within range, so are you'. From my father."

"Five second fuses usually last three," quipped Jonathan.

'Jonathan and Alexis have played this game together before,' thought Jim. Then he said out loud: "If your attack is going well, you may have walked into an ambush."

"If what you are doing to kill the enemy seems stupid, but it works, it isn't stupid," added Alexis.

"Bravery is to be the only one who knows you are afraid," said Jim.

"Wait your turn, handsome," Alex gently scolded. "But that is an excellent one, coming from the bravest man I know," she added in a very sincere tone.

"Nothing is better for the morale of the troops than to see a dead general every once in a while," mumbled Jonathan in a hurt but competitive way.

"Now, *that* is the best one yet," exclaimed Jim excitedly, sensing the tone of Jonathan's response.

"Too competitive for you two," concluded Alexis. "But here is one last good one — 'friendly fire, isn't'."

They laughed and the game was over.

'What did Alexis mean with her 'friendly fire' comment?' both Jonathan and Jim thought.

'I am not going to suggest that game again with these two,' Alexis thought to herself as she got up from the overly small kitchen table.

Chapter 53

October 1944

Just two weeks earlier, Jim was gone to Cuba for a week of tent meetings, an evangelistic crusade. He was the main speaker and had worked on his sermons and Bible studies for over a month. Jim was excellent in planning, managing, and making sure all was done to perfection. When you were non-catholic missionaries in a ninety-percent Catholic country, any poor planning or other weakness will be used to laugh the American missionaries out of town. The young Reverend Billy Graham and Jim's father, the Reverend Henry Barclay, were guest speakers. Jim did all the translating during the English sermons for the other speakers. It was a huge and very meaningful event.

The first weekend after Jim had flown out to Havana, Alex and Jonathan had dinner on one of the balconies of his residence at the hotel. It was a beautiful night, the breeze off Lake Maracaibo made the outside evening even tolerable. On a Friday the scrambled but muffled noise coming from cars, buses, and the downtown trolly, as well as the planned and the spontaneous street parties below, was the South American way of life, or what Jonathan called a typical Friday's "symphony of confusion and relief that the work week was over."

Alex was wearing a very light, yet opaque, long and breezy cover-up dress. She had arrived in dainty Italian sandals and was now in bare feet. The two maids, the chef, and the military aide were all in white garb. Jonathan was wearing linen tan pants, French dark brown sandals, and a masculine white silk shirt only buttoned halfway up. Each of their tans were golden — they had spent the afternoon riding their horses under the blazing Caribbean sun and periodically in and out of the water. It had been just a perfect afternoon. And now, after all that, and a lengthy siesta in their individual hammocks tied between palm trees along the water, this fabulous dinner and wine arrived.

"How do the others live?" asked Jonathan with a soft laugh.

Alexis' eyes scolded him pretty well, and he never made that joke again; never again.

"As we talked a couple of times before, Jonathan, things are getting confusing again," challenged Alex.

"I know, but do we have to talk about it now?"

"If not now, when, Jonathan?"

"You are right."

"Alex, are you here in Venezuela as a 'spy'?" asked Jonathan very seriously.

Alex looked directly at Jonathan and remained silent.

'What a silly question to ask,' thought Alex. 'Not, every housewife knows what she knows or knows weaponry and killing as she does … or even carries herself as she does.'

Eventually, Alex responded: "If you feel you have to ask, then the answer is 'no'. If you follow your instincts and what you were trained to act on, the answer is 'yes' … and I will have to kill you. By the way, all your weapons of choice are unloaded and in the cabana shower as we speak."

She slapped him, gently. And, with a twirl she was covered by her large scarf, and waved goodbye as she headed to her car.

Chapter 54

Brazilian, Peruvian, or Ecuadorian Amazon
November 1944

"Very intensely dark," Jim said to himself quietly. "Very intense."

It was noon above the jungle canopy, in this, the world's largest rain forest. 3.1 million square miles in size, covering about forty percent of the South American continent. And the Amazon includes parts of eight South American countries — Brazil, Colombia, Peru, Ecuador, Bolivia, Guyana, Surinam, and a French protectorate named French Guiana. All of this is twice the size of the African rain forest in the Congo.

And then, of course, there is the constant buzz from the insects and other creatures doing their thing. Every once-in-a-while you will hear a parrot or other bird calls. Finally, at night, the buzz turns to a drone from millions of cicadas.

Alex had learned that there were over three-hundred-and-ninety billion trees in the Amazon, from sixteen thousand different species. She loved trees.

And in all this largesse, Jim had pointed to the pilot to "just put us down there." 'There' was a small strip of what appeared to be hard sandy beach. Tiger, the pilot, was gone before the party had laid down their last bag. That was the last time in six hours that the three had seen the sky.

Hot up there, wet and cool down where the three were.

Jim felt the world on his shoulders, and in a small way to the world, but in a big way to him, it was, indeed, 'very intense'.

Here he was, an almost newlywed husband and wife, plus a Venezuelan and a German, chopping their way through the jungle brush in either Brazil, Peru, or Ecuador. Nobody knows because there are no marked and registered national borders where they were at the moment. They were dropped off three miles back in who knows where. 'They will never find us if things do not work exactly perfectly,' Jim thought. Three miles of truly virgin Amazonian jungle is like one hundred miles of straight clean pathway — maybe longer.

Lots of complaints from the Major, but absolutely none from Alexis. The Major had slipped and fallen several times into the lush vine-covered jungle floor and demonstrated how quickly he could get back up.

"Are you afraid of what is down there, or just embarrassed?" Alexis had asked after about the fifth time.

"Both," answered the ex-Nazi, "and I swear what I thought was a large log moved out of my way. And then, of course, there is the constant never-ending buzz from the billions of insects who call this home."

Each spoke quietly for several reasons — there were mammals, snakes, bugs, bugs and bugs, spiders (tarantulas), and bad guys (including some Nazis), and Indians out there who all would each enjoy some of these folks' blood.

Just the other day, the American and German (with the American woman distracting the six thugs for just one second, and that is all it took) had killed six German thugs who had cornered the three at a restaurant in Maracaibo. The six bodies were just a few of the other poor Axis-power citizens done away with over the course of the last two years in South America.

And one last thing … the Indians here, some friendly and not, were the absolute best at camouflage. Mainly because they had so much to hide behind and in.

Figure 14: An indigenous Indian in the South American jungle.

Cheo and Jim looked at each other and nodded.

"We will stop here for tonight," Jim stated. "There are plenty large branches to sleep on here, I count five in these two trees."

Jim continued to point.

"Cheo, would you please fix climbing pegs on that one there for her royal highness? We three can use our ropes," Jim added.

"Alex, you know this from our studies, but just as a reminder: all the ground and tree frogs come out at night. They are beautiful, but do not try to touch them. They are very toxic, and you will not be able to walk tomorrow. If they get on you, and they will, just let them do their thing. Ok?" Jim asked as if Alexis or any of the other three had a choice in this matter.

Jim and Cheo did most of the work, and Jonathan tried to help. However, Jonathan was a very out-of-place Bavarian elite — by no means not able to take care of himself and all the others if necessary — but, fortunately, it was not necessary.

'Cute but awkward,' Alexis thought as she looked at Jonathan. 'Whereas Jim just seems to fit in as if he was messing around in the street 'jungles' at night in Pontiac and Detroit.'

Cheo and Jim helped Alexis and Jonathan to their branches, and tried to explain that they may not fall asleep, but they must rest. With the snakes, frogs, and insects wanting to sleep on the same branches, the strangers from out of town needed to stay alert. Alexis and Jonathan were lectured by Jim about sleeping facing the trunk of the tree, in an attempt to see what was coming for them from this jungle home of others, and to be sure to tie themselves tightly on the branch as they were taught by Cheo.

Jim tried a joke that the fall from the limb to the soft jungle floor would not hurt or kill them, but whatever was sleeping on the ground below them would. I like that one … but Alexis and Jonathan did not.

This mission by the four was probably their most critical of the war. Several matters were coming together at once at this most remote place in the world.

The Nazis, still convinced there was Incan gold out here somewhere (and they were correct), wanted to come together and compare notes (or so said the your-eyes-only note to Jonathan from the Nazi powers that be); the transportation of tons of natural rubber sheets from Manaus, Brazil, down the Orinoco (rather than the Amazon, because the English Navy was only watching out for transport coming down the Amazon into the Atlantic) to ports in Nazi-controlled France, and even Tokyo, Japan. Italy was on the run early in the war; they had no more submarines and had stopped making tanks and trucks by early 1943, and the country was therefore the only of the three Axis powers not desperately in need of natural rubber, as opposed to the synthetic rubber Germany had been making even before it started the war in 1939.

And then, of course, there was one more item on the jungle-Nazi group's agenda — which nobody of this team of four knew — and it was that, again, the Nazi powers-that-be knew their secrets were getting out, and it could only be one of two or three suspects on the inside.

The leading suspect was Major Jonathan Speer — why not? The Nazis killed his dear Chloe, his younger and mentally challenged eight-year-old sister. These men knew that if this meeting were called, the uninvited Jonathan Speer would be there — that is who Jonathan is. His cousin knew him well — and he was there for the kill — that is what he was brought up by the Nazi Youth to be. Hitler first. State second. Family, at most third. God? What or who is God? Oh yeah, Hitler is God.

The four were in a tight-knit group of branches, and, whether by divine inspiration or chance or Alex' doing — the branch Alex slept on was between Jim and Jonathan, close enough to see each other. It would be interesting to have insight into their minds as they each laid there with their thoughts (and, snakes, insects, and poisonous frogs roaming about).

At dawn, the four were ready to complete the trek toward Manaus. The mission remained simple — at least regarding the goals.

There was allegedly a large boat about to leave Manaus to go down a tributary to where that tributary feeds into the Orinoco River. Once in the Orinoco, the boat would be indistinguishable from all the other boats innocently using the Orinoco for standard jungle commerce.

This boat was special because it was filled to the brim with layers of finely sized natural rubber. The layers were believed to be on their way to the Axis submarines. As soon as these U-boats could no longer be located with sonar due to their rubber coating, it is believed that the war would be extended another two full calendar years.

And, of course, what boat headed to one of the Axis powers would not have many millions of dollars' worth of gold and gems onboard — for Hitler and his thugs.

The party of four was to destroy in any way possible or at a minimum divert the boat so that it failed to reach the Amazon.

Each member was equipped with a rifle, pistol, and dagger of their choice, two grenades, and a machete.

"Confirm DUC — Now!" Jim ordered.

It was not unusual for members of elite OSS killer-groups to have a pre-arranged 'pact in blood' between group members with regard to consequences of capture by the target enemy. This was such an OSS group. Each group member would do all she or he could do to avoid physical pain of the other, the outing-of-secrets-by-torture, and the ultimate success of the mission. No secret is safe from proper torture. If anybody knew about torture, the Nazis and their thugs certainly did.

DUC is the acronym for the above mentioned 'pact of blood' — standing for 'Death Upon Capture'. Each member knew that upon their capture, death from a team member could come at any moment and by any means. And that death is demanded by the captured. And, in most circumstances, that death is a gift, considering what would most certainly happen to the captured at the hands of the captors.

"Confirmed!" said Alexis.

"Confirmed!" said Jonathan

"Confirmed!" said Cheo.

"Confirmed!" said Jim, adding "All confirmed!"

"Act quickly," Jim demanded of all. "If a member is captured, you must kill. There may not be a second chance, and the enemy knows about these pacts. They will protect the captured member from your team members! Act!"

Jonathan asked for point, and Jim acquiesced reluctantly. Jonathan was not an expert in jungle fighting as Cheo and Jim were. But, often the weakest is placed at point — that is just the way war is. Protect your strength, and in this battle to come, the strength of this team is Alexis, Cheo, and Jim.

The team quietly headed north toward Iquitos.

They must destroy the planned shipment of natural rubber to U-boat ports-of-call in the south of France.

Not doing so was estimated to extend the end of the war for two more years. Countless lives were at stake, not only military men and women, but the millions of helpless men, women, and children of all ages targeted by the Nazi regime and the Japanese Empire.

Chapter 55

Brazilian, Ecuadorian, or Venezuelan Jungle
End of November 1944

"There she is, folks," Jim whispered to the other three.

Before them was the so-called boat they were searching for in this awful jungle. It was moored close-by. Thankfully it was more of a barge than a boat. Guards were everywhere. The assumption had to be for each guard you could see, there were two others not visible.

"I bet their scouts just figured out the danger of the rapids just below here," Jim whispered.

"You know these parts that well?" Jonathan asked in amazement.

"Jonathan, much of the time your old Nazi friends could not figure out where I was, if they had been here, they would have found me. Yes, I have been here many times and I am also aware of the danger the rapids would cause that ugly and un-manageable barge if they dared to try getting through.

"All we have to do is cut the barge free, and just let it hit the rapids on its own. There will be very little left of the boat or its contents when pieces of it reach the Orinoco," Jim continued.

Cheo had already seen where Jim was going with this conclusion and was stripping naked. Jim was also undressed in a second and, with a motion, Cheo and Jim were helping each other in the murky Amazonian waters toward the barge.

Figure 15: The barge loaded with rubber being destroyed in the rapids of the Orinoco river.

"All they have to do?" Jonathan whispered to Alex.

"He has done this before, or at least Jim said he had. He knows the dangers of this water — undertows, crocodiles, piranha, snakes, and so forth. He also knows if anybody can do this, it's those two as a team." Alexis said between prayers asking God for success of this latest mission.

Minutes turned into an hour, and then another hour.

Suddenly, all hell broke loose across the river.

The barge was lazily and happily heading down the tributary and each of those yelling knew there was nothing they could do to avert destruction — many of the guards on the barge threw off their clothes and jumped into the river. 'These soldiers from Europe have very little chance of survival,' thought Alex.

Just as Alexis was about to ask Jonathan if he saw Jim and Cheo, before her stood a naked and wet American and a Venezuelan, each smiling from ear to ear.

"Yes!" said Jim to his team.

"Let's get out of here fast!" suggested Cheo as he and Jim gathered their belongings, checked their weapons, and got ready for battle.

Again, Jim let Jonathan take point. All he had to do was let Jonathan go anywhere except back to where all the yelling was coming from. Once they got further away, Cheo would take point and get the team out.

After a distance, Jim did check.

"Alex!" Jim softly challenged.

"Here!" was the response from fifteen yards behind Jim.

"Aqui!" was the response from twenty-five yards behind Jim.

No response from fifteen yards ahead.

"Point! Check!"

"Jonathan!" Jim challenged again, this time in more of a yell.

Alexis' heart pounded hard and sank even faster. She said nothing. Jim knew what Alex was thinking, and Jim and Cheo were just as concerned.

"Gather!"

Cheo and Alex hurriedly joined Jim.

"They have Jonathan — somehow they, or quiet Indians, got him. This was a trap! How did I not see this! Our only choice is to catch up to them and get Jonathan back immediately. Now that they know we are here, we are in attack-and-find mode. Their Indian friends are watching our every step. Let's go get Jonathan back — now. Follow me, go ahead and shoot at anything you think needs shooting at, and be ready for it to shoot back! Alex, take right one yard behind and three yards to the right. Cheo, to the left, same distances. We are now in battle mode — and we will come out the other side with Jonathan with us."

Jim left out '… or not come out at all.'

One of the many fine arts of jungle fighting is knowing the sounds of when your bullet hits flesh, a tree, a bunch of moss, or anything else. Another is to fall quietly and hide if you are hit. The men they were fighting against were not experts — you heard the bullet hit, you heard the grunt in pain, and the call for help or mother.

Suddenly, there was an opening, and the sound of airplane engines. Two engines — Tiger, thought Jim in disgust. A double agent going to the highest bidder. He would be the first Jim would knowingly kill today if given the chance.

"Cheo, it's Tiger and his Mosquito plane. Try to get close enough to shoot at it and hopefully kill the pilot. Go!"

With a knowing nod, Cheo was gone.

Jim grabbed Alexis and they headed to an old army-ant hill about two hundred yards from the roaring plane.

A group was quickly trying to go onboard — and one man was being pushed and shoved toward the plane door.

Jim grabbed his Garand rifle and aimed at the group. He was looking for Jonathan! He knows too much! They will get it out of him! Alexis is in danger if he speaks! Cheo and I are already in danger with what they know! They will torture Jonathan for days before they kill him!

We agreed what to do! We all knew what we were getting into.

Jim aimed at the head of the person being shoved into the plane.

'Do it Jim!' — Jim's mind screamed.

"Jim, you must do it now! We each asked for it. Would you shoot me? Do it!" yelled Alex.

"They are shoving him back and forth. Now only his back!" Jim whispered anxiously and tensely.

Alexis looked straight ahead. She could not see over Jim's shoulder. "Do it!! Nobody else here looks like that from the … [BANG] … back!"

Cheo had just returned and folded Alex into his chest. A deep and caring hug and Alex whimpered, but only for a second.

"Cheo — one pistol each. Carry pistol ammo anywhere you can. We are out of here. Now! We are running for our lives … know this and act like it … because it is very true!" gasped Jim. "Follow me as closely as each of you can, and still keep your speed."

Alex had never seen Jim's face so angry and sad.

Chapter 56

Maracaibo, Venezuela
December 1944

Alexis' mind was racing. Her heart, soul, and body felt completely drained. She had never felt like this.

'And the funeral! Probably the most difficult thing she has ever had to do,' Alex thought.

"Never again will I …" she said quietly to herself as the wind-noisy car weaved along the coast of the Caribbean. To her, it will never again be 'beautiful and enchanting', nor 'Buenos Aires, the Paris of South America'. Or, for that matter, Paris would never be Paris again.

What a tragic Shakespearian loss!

Alexis knew Jim had to kill him, but did he really *have to* kill him?

The rubber never made it to the Orinoco or to the mouth into the Atlantic.

'One … no, the only good thing out of all this,' Alexis thought to herself.

She truly loved both Jim and Jonathan, but she stayed loyal to her driver, Jim. At the funeral, however, there was no way in her mind to make that distinction. That really bothered her.

The road was curvy, just like the roads along the coast of New England. Alex's father always drove these curves with the passion of a race car driver. Jim, on the other hand, more like a confident, rhythmic and strong Latin dancer. And that is how he was driving today, aware that Alex was drained and feeling ill.

'He did everything lovingly for her,' Alex thought. 'Of course, her father loved her too, and teased her — like driving crazy. Jim did not tease.'

The international long-distance phone call to Alex at the small and elegant hotel was scheduled for 6:00 p.m. Caracas time. And the hotel was only about an hour's drive from the noon funeral. Jim loved the charming little 'secret' hotel — unadvertised seclusion for the rich and famous — and Jim and Alexis. They had been here before.

The November summer breeze coming off the salt water was trying to comfort Alex, so she rolled the window down all the way. Jim slowed down even further so Alexis could enjoy and relax.

"I am sorry, honey," Jim said tenderly, just loud enough for Alex to hear over the breeze. "You know he meant so much to me as well. Our working relationship ... 'it' was so special. A dear, dear friend."

But Jim knew 'it' was something more for Alexis.

"So much for God and Country," Jim scolded himself as his teeth clenched, his brain sped, and his hands gripped the steering wheel like he was going to rip it off the column. He truly loved Jonathan.

'Dear friend,' Alex thought. She knew that Jim knew, so she need not say any more. "It's over," she said to herself as she closed her eyes.

Chapter 57

Undisclosed Location, Venezuela
December 1944

Jim signaled the doormen to stay back and reached to assist Alex out of the car. 'He never let the doormen do their job,' Alex thought.

She loved how Jim treated and respected her — always. He worshiped her, kind of like Sir Francis Drake and Queen Victoria. Sir Francis never took Queen Victoria's affection for granted, and he worked feverishly and cleverly to retain it, and sometimes regain it. Jim did not have to work feverishly for his Queen. And she did not have to do anything to retain his affection.

Alex was Jim's, and Jim was Alex's. She knew it. He knew it. And they both knew the other knew it. "Done," Alexis said to herself.

As Jim tipped the bellman, Alexis surveyed the expansive yet inviting suite and the brilliance of the ocean streaming through the large east and north windows. The bed was opened slightly on both sides, the down blanket and extra woven soft cotton sheets looked seductively inviting, and the rose was on the pillow on her side. Always there, and always white.

The cozy small sitting area was just off to the right. And there was the phone. It began to ring. And it was exactly 6:00 p.m.

"Jim here," Jim said as he picked up the phone. He always started talking before the phone reached his ear.

"Mr. Barclay," said the familiar voice of the front desk manager.

"Thank you, Alfonse," Jim said with a sincere and respectful voice.

"You are welcome, sir. It is always a shame that with such a beautiful woman, you ask for coffee and tea rather than champagne and strawberries like all the others. I know, you are far from being …"

"… like the others," Jim murmured as he completed the sentence. They always played this little game. Jim enjoyed being known as 'not like the others'. His son was the same and learned this and many other fine things from his dad Jim — except I always used a yellow rose.

Jim knew that Alfonse was a French Vichy sympathizer. He was close to the German Nazis, but appeared not to take sides. The Vichy State was a consequence of the German — French Armistice of June 10, 1940. Germany ran the northern half of France, and the Vichy ran the Southern half along with the French colonies. Like any Vichy supporter, Alfonse would accept the ideology of whichever side would benefit him. Jim just hoped that he would not be put in the position of having to terminate Alfonse, but he would if required to fulfill the mission of his government.

Under most circumstances, Jim did not need the champagne for his many ventures with Lexi. It would be a while before either considered engaging in these ventures, thought Jim — just too sad a time.

"A call for Mrs. Barclay this time … from New York … it is unusually clear," Alfonse stated in a matter-of-fact way.

'Always, so many overseas calls for Suite 4A when Mr. Barclay is here,' Alfonse thought.

"Good," Jim said thankfully as he handed the phone to Alex.

"Hi again, Alfonse. Did you pick the rose?" Alex asked graciously of her host.

"Yes angel, and I carefully nurtured it as it grew … just for you." Alfonse was a wonderful flirt, as was Alex, and as are most men and women from the Spanish-speaking world.

"Then it should have been blue, Alfonse. We have had a rough day," she said.

"I am sorry, Mrs. Barclay. You should know only happiness, all the time. Maybe this phone call will help. It is Dr. Gentry … you know … the famous archeologist. She stayed here once!" Alfonse exclaimed. "But," he added, "not in Suite 4A, and no white rose."

"Thank you so much for your loving care, Alfonse," Alexis responded. "Let's get Carol on the line."

By 1941, Carol Fisher was the first world-famous female Cambridge-educated archeologist focused only on South America. She and Alex were best of friends, but Carol could never figure out why Alex married a missionary rather than the bankers-, lawyers-, and medical doctors-to-be who had tried to win over Alexis Hart. However, Carol always thought that she would have married Jim if she had met him first.

Carol always felt that there was something unique and special about Jim, ever since High School in Pontiac under the 'kissing tree'; but she could not lay her hands on it. However, she had observed over the years that Jim always was, without a doubt, a quiet and effective romantic. He always knew what to do … and not to do. But he did not drink!

"Hi Goldilocks," Alex said. Alex always thought Goldilocks was prettier than she because of the thick blond hair. She was not … but close.

"So, are you ready? Is Jim right there?" Carol asked excitedly.

"Yes, I am ready, and yes, Jim is right here, but about to give me some privacy," Alexis responded as she respectfully signaled Jim away.

Neither Jim nor Alexis ever shooed each other away.

"What are your conclusions?" mother asked.

"OK, I put things down in bullets like I always do, so here goes," Carol said.

'Bullets again, and today,' thought Alex.

"Alright, I am ready," Alex directed.

"First, the symbols on the locket direct the reader to the 'doily' you shared with me, not to any location of the 'material'." 'Material' was mother's code word for gold, and 'doily' meant the quipu that Jonathan had given mother. Only Carol knew this.

"However, and second," Carol softly and excitedly stated. "The material is not in Peru. It's not Peruvian. It's German!!!! Think stolen!!!"

"Alexis! It is a lot of material. I mean a lot!" Carol emphasized.

"Keep going Goldi," mother calmly scolded. "Keep going, but slowly."

"Slowly is hard, Alexis! What you dropped off over a month ago is incredible. Sorry it took so long."

"And finally, Alexis, you bossy woman you … the necklace clearly provides the latitude, longitude, geographical marking and more on where that material is located."

"Wow," Alexis said steadily.

"Yup," responded Carol.

"I said 'finally' to you, Alexis, but there are two more things." Goldi teased. She refused to let the funeral ruin this day for her or Alex.

"What? What?" Alexis said with little patience.

"Ok .. . I have to run, and we can talk in real detail at the Waldorf in three weeks. No talking to anybody about this, Alexis. Neither you nor I. Nothing! You understand?" said Carol.

"Yes! Absolutely! Nothing! But you said two things. Hurry!"

"Alexis," responded Carol, "the material is close to where you are right now!"

For the second time today, Alex felt overwhelmed.

"Oh my, too much to think about, and you said two," Alex stated impatiently.

"The person buried today was not your Jonathan. He is here in New York. We had lunch at the Plaza, and he said there is much for you and him to talk about, and he will meet your flight at La Guardia." Carol exclaimed excitedly.

Figure 16: Alexis realizing that Jonathan is still alive.

"Alexis?"

"Alexis?"

Alex had dropped the phone and fell softly against the silk-covered love seat, and then slipped gently to the soft alpaca rug on the floor. She just laid there, eyes open, and curled up with the pillow on the floor.

"So *that* is what Jonathan meant," she whispered to herself.

She tingled and, for the first time since the jungle around the Orinoco, smiled.

Jim knew nothing about what was said on the phone, but of course he knew about the material and where it was.

He also knew that Jonathan was alive.

Alexis had no idea that Jim knew any of this, and she did not even care about what others knew or did not know.

She was in her own world now.

Without a word, Jim hung up the phone.

And then, finally, so did Alfonse ... and he smiled in his devilish way.

The End

As with any relationship on this earth — between nations, races, individuals, those with resources, and those without, and the list could go on and on — there were significant tensions in the Jim-and-Alexis relationship. Sure, they were serving God, but so did the Old Testament Jonah and Job!

As I approached the end of this book, I noticed the absence of the very real and often enormous conflicts in the Jim-and-Alexis marriage. Mother kept *all* her notes from dad, and, maybe defensively, dad kept *all* of the notes from mother. The great majority were efforts to convey love in very difficult times. Unlike many young brides, my mother could not just pick up the cell phone and FaceTime her family for support to take her side. Although mother was busy, and busy with things many young brides may dream of, she was nonetheless alone. I was going to incorporate some of the notes Alexis delivered to Jim and Jim to Alexis — and a few from Alexis to Jonathan, particularly as the two aged — but without experiencing what each was dealing with, I could not come even close to such a summation.

I have a few favorite songs, and I love music as my mother and dad did. Music is a source of sharing that can flow between so many humans in tough situations. The most simple yet complex songs about struggling relationships is from one of my four favorite artists, Ricky Martin (the other three are Alejandro Sanz, Sting, and Elton John).

The title of the song in Spanish is Tiburones (sounds like 'tee-boo-rhonn-eehzz', and it translates to 'Sharks'). Below are the Spanish words, followed by the rough English translation.

Ya no sé por qué peleamos así
Basta de *hacernos* daño, que se nos van los años
Imposible que te *largues* así
Quédate aquí otro rato, vamos a *mojar* los labios

Es que no es que nos queremos
Que *nuestros* corazones
No les *gusta* estar a solas
Que nos mata el *sentimiento* y nos *sobran* las razones

Gastemos *todas* las municiones
Ganemos la batalla, que aún *queda* tiempo
Dale, vamos a *echar* el resto
Pero *cambiemos* el escenario que no *quiero* pelear *contigo* ¿Cómo la ves?

Vamos a *cambiar* de casa, *vamos* un mes de viaje
Hablemos otro idioma, bésame aquí en la calle

Por ti *cruzo* la tierra, *lucho* con mil leones
Por ti hago lo que sea, nado con tiburones

Vamos a *hacernos* una cena, una *noche* de vela con una *botella* del *mejor* vino
Vamos a *abrirnos* y *derribar* todos los *muros* con un *mismo* latido
Vámonos al cine, *leamos* un libro, *juntos* de la mano
Como dos locos, *vamos* de a poco, vamo' a *borrar* todo el pasado

Es que no ves que nos queremos
Que *nuestros* corazones
No les *gusta* estar a solas
Que nos mata el *sentimiento* y nos *sobran* las razones

Gastemos *todas* las municiones
Ganemos la batalla, que aún *queda* tiempo
Dale, vamo' a *echar* el resto
Pero *cambiemos* el *escenario* que no *quiero* pelear *contigo* ¿Cómo la ves?

Vamos a *cambiar* de casa, *vamos* un mes de viaje
Hablemos otro idioma, bésame aquí en la calle
Por ti *cruzo* la tierra, *lucho* con mil leones
Por ti hago lo que sea, nado con tiburones

Vamos a *cambiar* de casa, *vamos* un mes de viaje
Hablemos otro idioma, bésame aquí en la *calle*
Por ti *cruzo* la tierra, *lucho* con mil leones
Por ti hago lo que sea, nado con *tiburones* (por ti hago lo que sea)

(Hah-ah-ah) woh-oh-oh
(Hah-ah-ah) woh-oh-oh
(Hah-ah-ah) nado con tiburones
(Hah-ah-ah) woh-oh-oh
(Hah-ah-ah) woh-oh-oh

(Hah-ah-ah) yeah, tiburones
And, the English translation —

I do not know why we fight like this anymore
Let's stop hurting "us", as our years slip us by
Impossible for you to distance yourself like this
Stay here a while longer, and let's get our lips moist
With wine.

Can't you see we are truly in love
That our hearts are made for each other
They do not like to be alone
It destroys the "us" we want to be.

There are reasons to push all this aside
There is still time to get rid of the clutter
Let's change the scenery. Let's change whatever.
What do you think?

I do not want to fight with you
Let's change houses
Let's take a month-long unplanned trip
Let's talk in another language
Kiss each other here in the street
Let's enjoy each other.

We struggle on land with our own lions
We struggle at sea with our own sharks
But whatever we end up to be,
We will get there together.

Let's take time for a candlelight dinner
With a bottle of our favorite wine

Let's open the bottle, and
Raise our glasses to others as we.

Let's hold hands, as we once did
Let's go to the movies
Let's read a book together
If for no other sentiments,
If for no other reasons, other that
We know that our hearts cannot beat without the other.

So, let's …⁵
[repeat]

   My parents loved each other deeply — they nurtured each other and their relationship soundly … wanted what was best for the other and both purely … and led meaningful lives, loving lives, surviving together.

---

⁵ You can find video of Ricky Martin singing the song, changed a little for the times, at https://youtu.be/htWTuVOapXk, accessed 8 July 2023.

Epilogue

In June 1951, an impressive number of gold bullion bars were delivered to the mountain vault of the Industrial Bank of Switzerland (IBS). Each bar had the Nazi insignia and Hitler's signature inscribed. This vault, although significantly modernized today, has a private landing strip to service their ultra-net-worth clients from around the globe. Incredible.

What is even more incredible is that, years later, there were three very low-key hacks of the same mountain vault's super-secret electronic asset protection systems, in 1999, 2009, and 2019. In each of these years, the vaults and related accounts of three separate high-ranking ex-Nazi German or ex-imperial Japanese vaults, and their related accounts, were reduced in value overnight by more than $US 7,000,000 each in gold bar inventory only, three accounts every ten years, affecting nine accounts in total to date. In each of these nine cases, and although Nazi gold bars were removed from these nine vaults, none of these bars were removed from the parent vault, meaning that the 'missing' gold bars remain somewhere within a vault or vaults within the parent vault (that's all IBS will disclose to whomever Swiss laws require them to give this information). Under Swiss banking law (and highly complex regulations), it is hard if not impossible to negate a prior Swiss government 'guarantee' that the sanctity of the vault and its contents within the parent vault will never be violated or broken.

I smile when I think of Zoe's potential involvement in the losses in value to those nine accounts.

Finally, a large room-vault at the Montevideo IBS branch also received deliveries of precious items that had clearly been stolen by the Nazis from those they had imprisoned or most likely terminated at death camps or on site around Europe and the world. These poor souls included, among others, persons of Jewish decent, gypsies, Poles, Russians, Romanians, Ukrainians, and others who the Nazis tagged as 'undesirables'.

I cannot go into detail of how my father and mother set everything up (how would I know?), but suffice it to say that my mother did disclose in her journals that the primary uses of any liquid assets were and are used to (i) return as many of the stolen items to the rightful owners, (ii) hunt down and punish those Nazis, Imperial Japanese, and other persons who participated in the atrocities in some way related to the melted gold and the stolen items (e.g., at the various death camps, and there were twenty such camps in Poland alone), places such as Hadamar (where Chloe was murdered), mass executions (such as at Babi Yar in the Ukraine, where approximately thirty-four thousand Jewish men, women, and children (that includes babies, yes, babies) were executed by bullet — once having been stripped naked and forced to lie face down in the dirt or on top of those already executed or pretending, for the moment, that they had successfully been executed), (iii) to provide health services to children of any heritage or race round the globe, (iv) and pay related expenses required to accomplish the above (including through bribes or other not so visible means). One more point: absolutely no expense is to be spared to catch and kill (not bring in for justice) those who directly or indirectly were involved with these heinous acts of ultimate cowardice. Oh, and not surprisingly, one other expense to complete bringing to the surface the remaining estimated one thousand gold bars signed by Hitler.

After first receiving her doctorate degrees from Oxford in Micro-Biology and Nano-Chemistry, my sister Zoe dedicated her life to assure the above was accomplished. There are stories of vengeance, punishment, revenge, personal dangers and triumphs that merit a related book titled *The Missionary's Daughter*. Zoe was even more wise, flexible, brilliant, and beautiful than my mother ("If that was even possible," my dad, and yes, even my mother, would say…). There is a special place in heaven for selfless workers for justice such as Zoe. Sadly, she died at seventy years of age of rheumatoid arthritis of the lungs in 2022.

There is so much work that remains to be done. And the funds available to do great things for children are so much larger. The money should never run out. Note that when the above-mentioned gold bars were deposited at the IBS mountain vault in 1949, gold was valued at $33.85 per ounce. The value per ounce today is approximately $1,938 … and rising.

I hope you enjoyed this book and further appreciate the coming book related to my sister Zoe's efforts mentioned above. These will be the only books I write related to the hell on earth created and nurtured by the German Nazis, and the Italian and Japanese Imperialists during WWII.

We cannot ever forget.

Humbly and most sincerely,

The son of James and Alexis Barclay, 2023

Figure 17: Alexis and James Barclay, circa 1945.

A Note about the Cover

It is my honor that my close friend Mike Gilger agreed to provide the cover painting of South America. Mike is known for his internationally published goldsmithing designs, as well as his oil paintings. He describes his artwork as 'photo realism' and abstract – i.e. primarily bright colors. Mike's family-owned store, located in downtown Ames, Iowa, is named "Gilger Designs", and his wife, two sons and daughter continue with the family's art-centered tradition.

Made in the USA
Monee, IL
15 January 2024

Figure 1: Alexis Hart Barclay, circa 1960